A Thousand Tomorrows

*Also by Karen Kingsbury
in Large Print:*

Oceans Apart
One Tuesday Morning
A Time to Embrace
A Treasury of Miracles for Women:
    True Stories of God's Presence Today

*Also by Karen Kingsbury and
Gary Smalley
in Large Print:*

Redemption
Remember

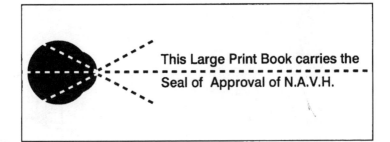

This Large Print Book carries the
Seal of Approval of N.A.V.H.

A Thousand Tomorrows

Karen Kingsbury

Thorndike Press • Waterville, Maine

Published in 2005 by arrangement with Warner Books, Inc.

Thorndike Press® Large Print Americana.

The tree indicium is a trademark of Thorndike Press.

The text of this Large Print edition is unabridged.
Other aspects of the book may vary from the original edition.

Set in 16 pt. Plantin by Elena Picard.

Printed in the United States on permanent paper.

Library of Congress Cataloging-in-Publication Data

Kingsbury, Karen.
    A thousand tomorrows / by Karen Kingsbury.
        p. cm. — (Thorndike Press large print Americana)
    ISBN 0-7862-7699-1 (lg. print : hc : alk. paper)
    1. Self-destructive behavior — Fiction. 2. Psychological
fiction. 3. Large type books. I. Title. II. Thorndike Press
large print Americana series.
    PS3561.I4873T48 2005b
                                                2005007579

Dedicated to . . .

Donald, my Prince Charming: The dance is a beautiful one; I only wish the music would play forever.

Kelsey, my forever laughter: Thanks for letting me into the most tender places of your heart.

Tyler, my sweetest song: When the spotlight hits you, honey, your dad and I will be there in the front row.

Sean, my silly heart: It feels like you've been in my heart forever.

Josh, my gentle giant: Our plan was two adopted Haitian boys; God's plan was three. I'm so glad He brought you to us.

EJ, my chosen one: Watching you come into your own, growing and stretching with the years, has been one of my greatest blessings.

Austin, my miracle boy: Your days are speeding by, precious youngest child. I can't slow the march of time, but you remind me I can savor every beat.

And to God Almighty, the Author of Life, who has — for now — blessed me with these.

As the Founder/CEO of NAVH, the only national health agency solely devoted to those who, although not totally blind, have an eye disease which could lead to serious visual impairment, I am pleased to recognize Thorndike Press* as one of the leading publishers in the large print field.

Founded in 1954 in San Francisco to prepare large print textbooks for partially seeing children, NAVH became the pioneer and standard setting agency in the preparation of large type.

Today, those publishers who meet our standards carry the prestigious "Seal of Approval" indicating high quality large print. We are delighted that Thorndike Press is one of the publishers whose titles meet these standards. We are also pleased to recognize the significant contribution Thorndike Press is making in this important and growing field.

Lorraine H. Marchi, L.H.D.
Founder/CEO
NAVH

* Thorndike Press encompasses the following imprints: Thorndike, Wheeler, Walker and Large Print Press.

Acknowledgments

Novels do not come together without a great deal of help. For that reason, I'd like to thank several people who helped make *A Thousand Tomorrows* possible.

First, a special thanks to Maureen Egen and Rolf Zettersten for taking me under your wing at Center Street and believing that maybe the whole world needed to know about this story. Your encouragement and faith in me have made all the difference. I appreciate you more than you know. Also, a thanks to my other friends at Center Street, especially my editor, Leslie Peterson, and my publicist, Andrea Davis. You are amazing in the way you think outside the box. I'm grateful beyond measure to be working with you.

Also, thanks to the people who helped lend credibility to this novel. A year ago, I shared a cross-country airplane ride with professional bull rider Ross Coleman. That four-hour conversation became the inspiration for Cody Gunner, the main character in *A Thousand Tomorrows*. Since that conversation, Ross Coleman and his family, along with dozens of rodeo competitors, cowboys, and professional bull riders including the all-time great Tuff Hedeman, helped make the world of rodeo real to me, and for that I am grateful. You lent accuracy to this story; any errors in detail are mine.

In addition, a thanks to those who shared their cystic fibrosis stories and information. I join you in praying for a cure for this disease, and for believing that in time research and funding will continue to add tomorrows every day.

Thank you to my family, especially Donald and the kids, who don't mind tuna sandwiches and quesadillas two weeks straight when I'm on deadline. You're the best support system I could ever have! Thanks also to my mother, Anne Kingsbury, who is my assistant and best friend. And a thanks to my dad, Ted Kingsbury, who continues to be my greatest encourager.

In addition I'd like to thank my friends and family who surround me with love and prayer and encouragement, especially Susan Kane, Trish Kingsbury, Lynne

Groten, Ann Hudson, Sylvia Wallgren, Sonya Fitzpatrick, Teresa Thacker, Kathy Santschi, Melinda Chapman, Christine Wessel, Vicki and Randy Graves, Marcia Bender, and so many others.

A special thanks to my agent, Rick Christian, at Alive Communications. You are brilliant at all you do, acting in so many roles as you lead me in this writing adventure. You care deeply about my career, but more than that, you care about me in my role as a wife and mother. Thanks for working out the details with that in mind. You're amazing, and I'm the most thankful author in the world to be working with you.

Chapter One

Mary Williams never saw it coming.

She became Mike Gunner's wife the summer of 1972, back when love was all the world needed, big enough to solve any problem. So big no one imagined it might end or die or drop off suddenly the way the muddy Mississippi River did ten yards out.

The wedding was small, held on a hillside in Oxford not far from Ole Miss, a stone's throw from the grassy football field where Mike had been king. Marriage, they told themselves, wouldn't mean losing their independence. They were just adding another layer to their relationship, something more diverse, more complex. As a reminder, during the ceremony they each held something that symbolized themselves — Mary, a book of poetry; Mike, a football.

A football.

Looking back that should've been a sign, because football was Mike's first love, and what sort of man could be married to two lovers? But at the time — with half the guests in flowing tie-dyed gowns and flower wreaths — holding a football and a book of poetry seemed hip and new, a spit in the face of tradition and marital bondage. No three-piece suits and starched aprons for Mike and Mary.

Mike had an NFL contract with the Atlanta Falcons, and a pretty new house a few miles from the stadium. Mary was a runaway, so leaving Biloxi meant cutting ties that were already frayed. They would live as one, him in a Falcons uniform, her with a pen and paper, ready to capture the deep phrases and rhymes that grew in the soil of her heart.

Babies? They would wait five years at least. Maybe ten. She was only nineteen, a child herself. Marriage would mean finding new and heightened ways to love each other. Sundays cheering from the stands while her husband blazed a trail down the football field, and lazy Tuesdays, barefoot and sipping coffee while she recited to him her latest creation.

That was the plan, anyway.

But God didn't get the memo, because Mary was pregnant three months later and gave birth to a baby boy shortly before their first anniversary. Cody William Gunner, they called him. Little Codester. Mary put away the pen and paper and bought a rocking chair. She spent her days and most nights walking a crying baby, heating up bottles, and changing diapers.

"Sorry I'm not around more," Mike told her. He wasn't used to babies. Besides, if he wanted to keep up, he needed more time at the field house, more reps with the weights, more hours on the track.

Mary told him she didn't mind, and the funny thing was, she really didn't. Life was good at home. Mike was happy about being a father, because Cody was all boy from the moment he was born. His first word was *ball,* and Mike bought him a pair of running shoes months before he could walk.

The years that followed were a blur of vibrant reds and happy yellows. Mike was coming into his own, each season showing him faster, more proficient at catching the long bomb. There had been no warning, no sign that life was about to fall apart.

In the spring of 1978, when Cody was nearly five, Mary learned she was expecting again. Still, it wasn't the coming baby, but a bad catch one October Sunday that changed everything. Mike was all alone, ten yards away from the nearest defender, when he reached for the sky, grabbed the ball and came down at an angle that buckled his knees.

A torn anterior ligament, the hospital report showed. Surgery was scheduled; crutches were ordered. "You'll miss a season," the doctor told him. "To be honest, I'm not sure you'll ever run the same again."

Six weeks later Mary gave birth to Carl Joseph.

From the beginning, Carl was different. He didn't cry the way Cody had, and he slept more than usual. His fussiest moments were during feeding time, when milk from the bottle would leak out his nose while he was eating, causing him to choke and sputter and cough.

Mike would look at him and get nervous. "Why's he doing that?"

"I'm not sure." Mary kept a burp rag close by, dabbing at the baby's nose and convincing herself nothing was wrong. "At least he isn't crying."

Either way, Mike wanted to be gone. As soon as he could, he got back in the training room, working harder than ever to make the knee well again. By the next fall, he was cleared to play, but he was more than a second slower in the forty.

14

"We'll try you at special teams, Gunner," the coach told him. "You've got to get your times down if you want your spot back."

His future suddenly as shaky as his left knee, Mike began staying out with the guys after games, drinking and coming home with a strange, distant look in his eyes. By the time Carl Joseph was two, Mike was cut from the Falcons. Cut without so much as a thank you or a good-luck card.

By then they knew the truth about Carl Joseph.

Their second son had Down syndrome. His condition came with a host of problems, feeding issues, developmental and speech delays. One morning Mary sat Mike down at the breakfast table.

"You never talk about Carl Joseph." She put her hands on her hips. "You act like he has the flu or something."

Mike shrugged. "We'll get him therapy; he'll be fine."

"He won't be fine, Mike." She heard a crack in her voice. "He'll be this way forever. He'll *live* with us forever."

It was that last part that caught Mike's attention. He said nothing significant at the time, nothing Mary could remember. But that summer, he was gone more than he was home. Always his story was the same. He was traveling the country looking for a tryout, getting a few weeks' look in one city and then another, working out with a handful of teams, trying to convince coaches he hadn't lost a step, hadn't done anything but get stronger since his injury.

But one weekend morning, when Mike was still asleep in their bedroom, Mary found a Polaroid picture in his duffle bag. It was of him in a bar surrounded by three girls, one on each knee, one draped over his shoulder.

When Mike woke up, Mary was in the kitchen ready to confront him. He would have to stop traveling, stop believing his next contract was a tryout away. Bars would be a thing of the past, because she needed him at home, helping out with the boys. Money was running out. If football had nothing more to offer, he needed to find a job, some other way to support them. She had her speech memorized, but it was all for nothing.

He took control of the conversation from the moment he found her at the kitchen table.

"This . . ." He tossed his hands and let them fall limp at his sides. His eyes were bloodshot. "This isn't what I want anymore."

"What?" She held up the Polaroid. "You mean this?"

Anger flashed in his eyes. He snatched the picture from her, crumpled it, and slammed it into the trash can. The look he gave her was cold, indifferent. He gritted his teeth. "What I do outside this house is my business."

She opened her mouth, but before she could tell him he was wrong, he slid his wedding ring from his left hand and dropped it on the table between them.

"It's over, Mary. I don't love you anymore."

Carl's cry sounded from upstairs. Slow and monotone, the cry of a child who would always be different. Mary looked up, following the sound. Then she found Mike's eyes again. "This isn't about me." She kept her tone calm, gentle. "It's about you."

A loud breath escaped his lips. "It's not about me."

"It is." She sat back, her eyes never leaving his. "You were on top of the world before you got hurt; now you're out of work and afraid." Compassion found a place in her voice. "Let's pull together, Mike." She stood, picked up his ring, and held it out to him. "Let me help you."

Carl's crying grew louder.

Mike closed his eyes. "I can't . . ." His words were a tortured whisper. "I can't stay here. I can't be a father to him, Mary. Every time I look at him, I . . . I can't do it."

Mary felt the blood drain from her face and the cheap linoleum turn liquid beneath her feet. What had he said? This was about Carl Joseph? Precious Carl, who never did anything but smile at Mike and long to be held by him?

Mary's scalp tingled, and the hairs on her arms stood straight up. "You're saying you can't stay married to me because of . . . because of Carl Joseph?"

"Don't say it like that." He pinched the bridge of his nose and hung his head.

Carl's crying grew still louder.

"But that's it, right?" The truth was exploding within her, spraying shrapnel at her heart and soul and leaving scars that would stay forever. "You want out because you can't be a father to Carl Joseph. Or because you're embarrassed by him. Because he's not perfect."

"I'm already packed, Mary. I called a cab; I'm flying to California and starting over. You can have the house; I'll send money when I get a job."

In a small, less important part of her mind, Mary wondered where Cody was, why he was so quiet. But she couldn't act on her curiosity. She was too busy reminding herself to breathe. "You're leaving because your son has Down syndrome? Do you hear yourself, Mike?"

But he was already headed back up the stairs.

When he left the house ten minutes later, he mumbled a single good-bye to no one in particular. Cody came tearing into the entryway from the living room, his eyes wide, forehead creased with worry.

"Dad, wait!" Cody ran out the door, his untied tennis shoes flopping with every step.

Carl Joseph in tow, Mary followed, horrified at the scene playing out. The cab waited out front, and without turning back, Mike helped the driver load both his suitcases into the trunk.

Cody stopped a few feet away, chest heaving. "Dad, where are you going?"

Mike hesitated, his eyes on Cody. "Never mind."

"But Dad —" Cody took a step closer. "When're you coming home?"

"I'm not." He looked at Mary and back at Cody. "This is it, son." Mike moved toward the passenger door. "Be good for your mama, you hear?"

"But Dad . . . I got a baseball game Friday; you promised you'd be there!" The boy was frantic, his words breathless and clipped. "Dad, don't go!"

Mike opened the door of the cab.

"Wait!" Mary stormed barefoot across the damp grass toward the cab. Carl Joseph stayed behind, rooted in one spot, watching, his thumb in his mouth. Mary jabbed her finger in the air. "You can't leave now, Mike. Your son's talking to you."

"Don't do this, Mary." Mike shot her a warning look. He lowered himself a few inches toward the passenger seat. "I have nothing to say."

"Dad!" Cody looked from Mike to Mary and back again. "What's happening; where're you going?"

Mike bit his lip and gave a curt nod to Cody. "Good-bye, son."

"Fine!" Mary screamed the word, her voice shrill and panicked. "Leave, then." She bent over, her knees shaking. Tears ran in rivers down her face. "Go ahead and leave. But if you go now, don't come back. Not ever!"

"What?" Cody looked desperate and

sick, his world spinning out of control. He glared at his mother. "Don't say that, Mom. Don't tell him not to come back!"

Mary's eyes never left Mike's face. "Stay out of this, Cody. If he doesn't want us, he can go." She raised her voice again. "Do you hear me, Mike? Don't come back!"

What happened next would be a part of all their lives as long as morning followed night. Cody's father looked once more at the three of them standing on the lawn, then he climbed into the backseat, shut the door, and the cab pulled away.

"Dad!" Cody screamed his name and took off running.

The sound frightened Carl Joseph. He buried his face in his hands and fell onto his knees, rocking forward and calling out, "Mama . . . Mama . . . Mama."

Mary went to him. "Shhh. It's okay." She rubbed his back. Why was this happening? And why hadn't there been any warning? She was dizzy with shock, sick to her stomach and barely able to stand as she watched Cody chase after his father's cab.

Never did the cab slow even a little, but all the while Cody kept running. "Dad! Dad, wait!" Five houses down, seven, ten. "Don't go, Dad! Please!"

Each word hit Mary like a Mack truck.

21

When she couldn't take another minute, she screamed after him, "Cody, get back here!"

But he wouldn't come, wouldn't stop running. All the way to the end of the block, with a speed he'd gotten from his father, he ran until the cab was long gone from sight. Then, for ten minutes, he stood there. A dark-haired eight-year-old boy, standing on the corner staring after a cab that wasn't ever coming back.

In some small way, Mary was almost glad Mike was gone.

Sure, a few hours earlier she'd been willing to fight for their marriage. But that was when she thought things were simpler. She could understand his confusion, what with his football career in limbo.

But to be embarrassed by Carl Joseph?

Carl was her son, a part of her. Because of his disability, he'd never be capable of the kind of low, mean-spirited act his father had just committed. No, Carl would always have a kind, simple heart, but Mike would miss that — the same way he'd missed everything about Carl Joseph since the day he was diagnosed.

Even as she stood there, willing Cody to turn around and come home, not quite believing her marriage was over, she felt her resolve building. There was no loving a man who didn't love his own son. If Mike didn't want to be a father to Carl Joseph, she'd love the boy enough for both of them. She would survive, even if she never heard from Mike Gunner again.

She focused on Cody once more, his little-boy shoulders slumped forward as he waited, facing the empty spot where the cab had disappeared. He was crying, no doubt. She could almost see his smudged, tearstained cheeks and the slack-jawed look on his face. Was he feeling the way she felt? Abandoned? Overcome with despair?

A strange thought hit her, and suddenly fear had the upper hand.

Because the thought was something she hadn't considered until that moment. Yes, she would survive, and certainly Carl Joseph would be okay without Mike. But Cody adored his father; he always had. And if the boy's slumped shoulders were any indication, Cody might not bounce back the way she and Carl would.

Rather, he might never be the same again.

Chapter Two

Cody's sides hurt from running.

He dug his fingers into his waist and stared down the empty street. "Dad!" The picture filled his mind again. The cab slowing down, stopping for a minute, then making a gradual left turn. "Dad, come back."

A breeze hit him in the face and he realized he was crying.

"Dad!" Cody gasped, grabbing at any air he could suck in. Why did he leave? Where did he go? Dad took trips all the time, but he always came home. Always. What had he said? He wasn't coming back; was that it? His dad's words rumbled around inside him, making his chest tight, filling his heart and soul and lungs with hurt. Every breath was a struggle.

His dad was gone.

He was gone and there was nothing Cody could do about it. *Come back, Dad!* The words stayed stuck in his throat this time, and he stared down. *Stay, feet. Don't move. He'll come back; he will.*

Cody lifted his eyes to the place where the cab had turned. Any second, right? He'd turn around, come back home, tell them all he was sorry for getting so mad, right? Cody waited and waited and waited. And then he remembered the thing his dad had said about Carl Joseph.

I can't be a father to him . . .

Eight years was plenty old enough for Cody to understand the problem. Carl Joseph was different. He didn't look right or talk right or walk right. He was happy and really good at loving everyone and he almost never got mad, but their dad maybe didn't notice that. That's why, this time, having his dad leave was more serious.

Because he didn't want to be a daddy to Carl Joseph.

Cody stared down the street. *Come back, Dad . . . turn around.* He waited and watched for a long, long time.

Nothing.

No movement, no sounds of cars turning around and coming back. No yellow cabs. Just the quiet dance of twisty green leaves above him and the hot summer song of unseen crickets. Or something like crickets.

Later his mother would tell him that she

cried for him, standing there all that time, waiting for his father to come back. But after a while, Cody wasn't just standing there waiting; he was swept up in a feeling he'd never known until that day.

It started in his feet, almost as if it were oozing up through the cracked bumpy sidewalk. A burning that flooded his veins and pushed higher, past his knees and thighs, into his gut, where it swirled and mixed and grew until it filled his heart and mind, and finally his soul.

Not until it fully consumed him, not until it took up every spare bit of his young body, did he realize what had come over him, into him.

Cody knew what hate was because of Billy Bloom in his second-grade class. Billy was bigger than everyone else. Bigger and meaner. He tripped kindergartners, and stole the ball from the kickball game at recess, and laughed at Cody when he got a wrong answer in math. Cody hated Billy Bloom.

But what he was feeling now, this was something new, something so powerful it burned in his arms and legs and made him feel heavy and slow and trapped. All the other times Cody had used the word hate, he'd been wrong. Because *this* —

what he felt for his father — was hatred.

Cody never told anyone, but that morning he felt his heart shrivel up and die, all except the piece that belonged to Carl Joseph. His little brother thought Cody was Superman and Christopher Robin all rolled into one. As the weeks passed, every morning was the same routine. Carl Joseph would scamper down the hall to Cody's room, slip inside, and stand next to the bed.

"Brother . . ." He would pat Cody's shoulder. "It's a new morning."

Cody would stir and blink his eyes and find Carl Joseph there. "Yep, buddy. A brand-new morning."

"Is Daddy coming home today?"

Cody would grit his teeth and sit up some. "Not today, buddy. I don't think so."

For a minute worry would cast shadows on Carl Joseph's face. But then a grin would fill his round cheeks and he'd make a funny chuckling sound. "That's okay, 'cause know why, brother?"

"Why?"

" 'Cause I have you, brother. I always have you."

Cody would hug him around the neck. "That's right, buddy. You always have me."

The two of them were inseparable. Carl Joseph followed him around the house, waiting for him at the front window on school days. He didn't talk as clear as other kids, and he had those puffy bunches of skin under his eyes. But he was the happiest little guy Cody ever saw. He loved with abandon, and after a few months he walked into Cody's room one morning and didn't ask about when Daddy would come home.

That day Carl Joseph worked his way into the deepest part of Cody's heart. He still wasn't sure exactly what was wrong with Carl Joseph, but whatever it was, Cody had a feeling there wouldn't be many people in his little brother's life. If their dad didn't want Carl Joseph, maybe no one would.

No one but Cody. Whatever else happened, Cody would love Carl Joseph, and maybe that was all he'd ever love. He had no use for his mother; she was a grown-up, the only one with the power to keep Cody's father home. Instead, she'd stood right there on the grass and told him to go. Told him to go and never come back.

The rest of that year, Cody would wait until Carl Joseph was asleep, then he'd creep up to his room without saying good

28

night to his mother. He'd lie on the bed and stare at the wall. Sometimes tears would come, sometimes not. Always he would start at the beginning.

Hearing his dad talk to his mom about leaving, about not wanting to be with Carl Joseph. Then seeing his dad with a suitcase and following him out into the front yard and watching him head for the yellow cab.

"Good-bye, son. Good-bye."

The story would run again and again in his head, playing out on the blank wall beside his bed. Almost always his mother would find him there. Most of the time she didn't ask about why Cody went to bed early or why he was lying on his side staring at the wall or why he never told her good night or what he was feeling about his dad being gone.

But once in a while she would try.

Cody remembered one night the next spring when his mom came up to talk to him. She opened the door and took a loud breath. Then she moved a few steps toward him. "I hate that you hide up here, Cody. You're not the only one hurting."

"Yes, I am!" Cody turned over and sat up. His heart skittered around in his chest. "Carl Joseph doesn't remember Daddy."

"I miss him, too." She sat on the edge of

his bed. Her eyes were red and swollen, and her voice was tired. "I love him, Cody. It's not my fault he left."

"It is too your fault!" Cody closed his eyes and remembered his father leaving. When he opened them the anger inside him was bursting to get out. "You told him to go!"

"Cody." His mom touched his foot. Her fingers were shaking. "I didn't mean it."

"Yes you did!" His voice got louder. "You told him to go and never come back."

"Because I was mad. I didn't really want him to go."

But nothing she said that night or any other time was enough to convince Cody. She told his dad to leave, and not only that, she did nothing to make him stay. Maybe if she'd been nicer to him, helped him find another football job. Made him better dinners. Anything to make sure he didn't walk out the door.

Even when it no longer made sense, long after his childhood days blended into middle school, Cody blamed her. Because it was easier to dole out blame than it was to unravel the knot of hatred and sort through the loose ends of a lifetime of bitterness.

By the time Cody was in seventh grade, the football coach approached him.

"You're Mike Gunner's boy, right? Atlanta Falcons back a few years ago?"

Cody bristled, his spine stiff. "Yes, sir."

"Well." The coach gave a few slow nods. "I've watched you out with the other boys." The man hesitated. "You're good, Cody. You play just like your dad. The varsity coach over at the high school wants you to join 'em for practice a few times a week. How does that sound?"

Cody made a hurried attempt at trying to sort through his emotions. *Just like my dad?* He swallowed, not sure what to say.

The coach raised his brow, as if maybe he expected a different reaction. "What can I tell 'em, Gunner? You interested?"

"Yes, sir." He coughed and his words got stuck in his throat. Was that why he loved the game, loved the way the ball felt in the crook of his arm, tucked against his ribs, the way his feet flew down the field? Because he was Mike Gunner's boy? The anger that lived and breathed in that dark closet of his heart roared so loud it took his breath away.

If football was his father's legacy, he wanted nothing to do with it.

The coach started walking away. "Okay,

then. I'll tell him you'll be there."

"Sir?" Cody's face grew hot. He waited until the coach turned around. "What I mean is, no, sir. I won't go; I'm not interested."

The coach gave him a strange look. Then he laughed. "Of course you're interested, Gunner." He twisted his face. "Football's in your blood."

"No, sir." Cody's mind raced, desperate for an answer. "I'm . . . I'm going out for band."

"Band?" The word clearly left a bad taste in the coach's mouth. "You're kidding, right?"

"No, sir." Cody tried to look serious. "I . . . I love band." He hesitated. He would no sooner go out for band than dye his hair pink. Cody felt himself relax; he stood a little taller. "Band's what I live for."

The coach studied him, a frown deepening the lines in his forehead. Then he shrugged and took a step back. "Suit yourself, Gunner. I'll tell 'em you have other plans."

As Cody watched the man leave, a certainty filled his soul. He would never pick up a football again as long as he lived. No matter his feelings for the game, if seeing him with a pigskin reminded people of his father, he wanted none of it.

Later that year he fell in with a group of 4-H kids, guys who needed help with their farming or livestock. Cody was a quick study, and after a few months he could handle a horse as well as the kids who'd been on them for years.

One night just before summer, he and the guys met at the fairgrounds to watch the high school rodeo team practice. They moved close to the fence and Cody breathed it in, the heavy smell of bull hides. Cody knew about bull riding, but that night was the first time he ever saw a cowboy ride. The guy was a junior, a scrawny kid Cody had seen around town. Slow and careful, the cowboy lowered himself onto a jet-black bull, and in a blur the gate flew open and the animal burst into the arena.

Wild and out of control, the bull bucked and jerked and reared his head back. It was all the cowboy could do to hold on, and after six seconds, he slid to one side of the animal's back and fell hard in a heap to the ground.

"No good!" an older cowboy shouted. The man was in his late twenties, maybe. The rodeo coach, no doubt. "You need eight, Ronny. Eight seconds."

The kid picked himself up, dusted off his loose-fitting jeans and pressed his cowboy hat onto his head. His voice held a type of respect Cody admired. "Yes, sir. Eight seconds."

Five bulls stood together in a stock pen. The black one, two brown, one gray- and white-spotted, and one that was broad and yellow with a hump between its shoulders. One after another Ronny and a handful of high school cowboys took on the bulls while their instructor shouted out advice.

"Find the seat, Taylor, find it and keep it! . . . Move your legs, Ronny. . . . Kevin, bring your hand up higher over your head! Okay, good."

Cody barely heard any of it.

He was too busy watching the bulls, studying them, hypnotized by their fury. Those eight seconds, while the cowboy was on the bull's back, were the picture of a battle he knew intimately. The war he waged every day against the anger and rage within him. The way the rider struggled to stay on through the violent bucking, looking for the center of a ride that was never even close to controlled. It was the same way he fought to stay on top of the emotions that boiled inside him.

Before he could voice what he was feeling, without saying a word to his buddies, he followed the fence around the arena and walked up to the man still barking orders at the cowboys.

"That's better, Ronny; can you feel it? Keep it centered!"

"Sir?" Cody squared his legs and crossed his arms.

The man gripped the crown of his hat and looked over his shoulder. "Whadya want, kid?"

Cody didn't hesitate. "I want to ride."

"Yeah?" The coach smiled and a sarcastic chuckle sounded deep in his throat. "What are you, eleven?"

"Thirteen." The anger grew a few degrees hotter. He straightened himself. "I'll stay on any bull you've got."

The man leaned into the fence and sized him up. "What grade you in? Seventh?"

"Yes, sir."

"Another year before you can ride for me." He turned toward the action in the arena.

Cody stared at the man's back and clenched his teeth. He didn't need anyone's permission to ride a bull. It was his own thing; between the bull and him. He continued around the arena to the chutes.

One of the cowboys shot him a look. "Hey, kid, get lost. This is for cowboys only."

"I'm a cowboy." He nodded the brim of his hat toward the coach. "He wants to see what I can do."

The kid frowned, but then his expression eased. He raised one shoulder. "Okay. Take the next one."

He should've been scared, at least. The bulls had no horns, but the animals were massive. One slip beneath those muscled legs, and there wouldn't be any ride to remember. Cody worked the muscles in his jaw. As long as the coach didn't see him in the chutes, he'd be all right.

When it was his turn, he glanced at the coach and felt himself relax. The guy was talking to three riders, his back to the chute. Cody held his breath. He wasn't leaving the arena without getting on a bull.

"Take your ride, little man," one of the bigger cowboys shouted at him. "We're waiting."

Cody bit down hard and steadied himself. Then he did what he'd seen the other cowboys do. He climbed into the chute, one foot on either side of the bull, and fumbled with the rope. His hand had to be wrapped to the bull somehow, right? He flipped the rope around, trying to make a loop.

"Oh, brother. Ain't you ever done this?" The cowboy on the gate leaned over. "Which hand you ridin' with?"

Which hand? Cody gulped and thrust his right hand out.

"That'll do." The cowboy set to work wrapping Cody's hand, palm up, until it was tight against the bull's back. "Slide forward."

Cody did as he was told. That's when he noticed the look in the bull's eyes.

Lifeless, hard eyes, trying to catch a glimpse of whichever mortal had dared climb on his back. Cody stared at the beast. The anger in the animal's expression was rivaled only by his own.

"Ya hear me, cowboy? You ready?"

Cody blinked. What was he doing, sitting on a bull? Was he crazy? Fear tried to say something, but anger kicked it in the shins. *Come on, bull, give it all you got. Your fury's nothing compared to mine.* He nodded. "Ready."

The chute was open.

Stay centered, wasn't that what the coach had told the other riders? *Keep your seat; stay centered.* He focused on the animal's back, and suddenly he wasn't fighting to stay on a bucking bull. He was taking on his father, battling the loneliness and rejection and abandonment, focusing all his rage on the beast.

How many times had thoughts of his dad made him want to punch his hand through a wall or rip a door from its hinges? Running helped some, but nothing eased the rage in his heart.

Nothing until now.

The buzzer sounded. Cody pulled his hand free and swung his legs over the side of the bull. Something was making its way through his veins, but it took a few seconds to realize what it was.

Relief.

For the first time since his father walked out, his heart didn't feel paralyzed with rage. The reason was obvious: he'd left every bit of emotion on the back of the bull.

Only then did he hear the coach bellowing in his direction. One of the cowboys herded the bull back into the chute, and a hush fell over the arena. Cody turned and stood frozen, facing the man. His buddies had moved closer. They were clustered outside the fence, eyes wide.

"Stay there, kid. Don't move!" Even in the shadowy arena lights, the coach's cheeks were bright red. He stormed up to Cody until their faces were inches apart. His voice fell to a dangerous hiss. "I told you to go home."

"Sorry, sir." Cody swallowed hard, but he didn't break eye contact. "I . . . I had to ride tonight. I *had* to."

The man twisted his face into a sneer aimed at Cody. Then, bit by bit, his face unwound and he took a step back. "Where'd you learn to ride like that?"

He couldn't lie to the man now; not if he wanted to ride again. "That was my first ride, sir."

"Your first . . ." The coach narrowed his eyes. "That was your first time on a bull?"

"Yes, sir." Cody pulled himself a bit straighter. "I'm sorry, sir."

The man hung his thumbs on his belt buckle. "What's your name, boy?"

"Cody. Cody Gunner."

"You going to Jefferson High, Gunner?"

"Yes, sir." He looked at the ground for a moment. "When I'm old enough."

"You wanna be a bull rider, is that it?"

A bull rider? Cody hadn't considered the idea before. But he wanted to climb back on a bull more than he'd ever wanted anything. Cody exhaled, still catching his breath, his eyes on the coach again. The rush from the ride was wearing off. "Yes, sir. I want that."

The coach hesitated. This was the part where he'd kick Cody out of the arena and tell him he'd never ride for Jefferson's rodeo team. Not ever. Cody waited, unable to blink under the man's stare.

But instead of ordering him home or threatening him for his actions, the coach gave a single nod. The hint of a rusty old smile tugged on his lips. "You know something, Cody Gunner? I think you'll be a pretty good one."

After that, there was no turning back.

Cody's birthday was three weeks later, in June. He wanted just one thing — tuition and transportation to a bull-riding school in Colorado.

"Bull riding?" His mother frowned. "Cody, that's the craziest sport on earth." She crossed her arms and tapped her foot. "You can do anything but that." She turned back to the dishes she'd been doing. "Play football like your daddy. At least then you'll go head-to-head with a boy your size. Not a bull."

Football like his daddy? Cody felt his gaze harden. He had nothing but contempt for his mother. After all this time she still didn't get it, didn't understand him. Sure, she was easy on him. She didn't give him rules the way other boys had rules from their parents. Instead she gave him whatever he wanted, and peppered him with questions. "Cody, how are you?" "Cody, what're you thinking?" "Cody, what are you feeling?" "Cody, what's wrong?"

He was sick of her questions, sick of her trying to make up for the fact that he didn't have a dad. She never hassled him about his attitude or lack of kindness, even when he secretly wished she would.

But if she could suggest football, she didn't even know him.

Carl Joseph must've heard the conversation because he pushed his way between them. He was eight by then, as sweet and simple as he'd been at two. "Cody, brother, c'mere!"

The heat in Cody's anger cooled. Carl Joseph was his best friend, the only one he could trust. Cody couldn't count the times he'd wished it were he and not Carl Joseph who'd been born with Down syndrome. Because at least Carl Joseph was happy, too simple to understand even that their father had gone away, let alone the reasons why. Carl Joseph's eyes were honest and full of light, and his enthusiasm knew no limits. He called Cody "brother," and

41

Cody called him "buddy."

Carl Joseph grabbed his hand and pulled. "C'mon, brother, talk to me."

"Just a minute, buddy." Cody glared at his mother. "It's Mom's turn."

"No, Cody!" Carl Joseph grinned big and tugged a little harder. His voice was loud, excited.

This time Cody couldn't resist. He gave his mother a look and let himself be pulled into the next room. When Carl Joseph thought they were alone, his eyes sparkled. "You gonna ride a bull, Cody?"

Cody's heart swelled at the transparent look in his brother's eyes. A look of thrill and pride and expectancy. "Yes, buddy. I'm gonna be a bull rider."

"Remember, brother? We watched bull riding on TV?" He rocked back and forth, nervous, anticipating.

"We sure did, buddy." Cody put his arm around Carl Joseph's shoulders and gave him a sideways hug.

Carl Joseph let out a whooping victory cry. He slid from Cody's grasp, marched his feet up and down and moved in a tight winner's circle around Cody. His arms punched at invisible targets. "Bull riding! Brother's gonna be a bull rider!"

As Cody watched Carl Joseph that familiar fierce protection reared up in his heart. Once, a few years after their father left, a kid in his class pointed at Cody and laughed. "*His* brother's a retard! He lives in my neighborhood."

Never mind that the kids were taking a spelling test. Cody had the guy pinned before he had time to cry for help. It took the teacher and a passing custodian to pull Cody off the boy. It was the last time anyone at Davis Elementary said anything mean about Carl Joseph.

Watching him now, the determination in Cody's heart grew. No one better ever harm Carl Joseph, not ever. His brother stopped, drawing loud, exaggerated breaths. "I'm tuckered out, brother."

Cody smiled. "Yeah, you look like it."

So what if his mother didn't approve? He'd already made up his mind. The fact that Carl Joseph was excited only made him that much more sure.

Cody brushed his knuckles along the top of Carl Joseph's head. "We'll talk later, okay?" He made a face. "Mom's waiting."

"Right." Carl Joseph nodded, and did his best imitation of Cody's grimace. "Mom's waiting."

Cody grinned. What wasn't there to love about Carl Joseph? He turned and found his mother waiting in the kitchen. Her arms were crossed.

"What was that all about?"

"Carl's happy for me." Cody stuck out his chin. "I'm fourteen in a few weeks, Mom. I wanna go to bull-riding school. That's all I want."

Her look said everything her words didn't.

She wanted to be mad, wanted to tell him all the things any mother would tell her son if he came home wanting to be a bull rider. People were killed riding bulls; trampled and maimed and paralyzed. A body could age four decades in as many seconds in a sport that violent and unpredictable. But she must've seen the determination in Cody's eyes, because she blinked.

And that single blink told Cody he'd won.

The arrangements came together quickly, and by the time he arrived home from bull-riding school, he couldn't think of anything but getting a seat on the next bull.

Quickly Cody learned something about bull riders. The very good ones rode because they loved the sport, because they'd loved it since they were old enough to jump on the back of a sheep. For those riders, every go-round was an unequaled adrenaline rush, an addictive high that knew no match.

Cody was nothing like those cowboys.

Through middle school and high school, past his eighteenth birthday when he qualified for his Professional Rodeo Cowboys Association card; through event after event when sheer fury drove him to stay on bulls that couldn't be ridden; through the first two seasons when he first noticed Ali, the first two seasons when people started whispering that maybe there was no better bull rider than the independent Cody Gunner and no better barrel racer than the untouchable Ali Daniels, through all the travel and women and rank rodeo stock, he couldn't get one thought out of his head:

His father walked out of Carl Joseph's life because the kid had Down syndrome, because something was clearly wrong with that son. Cody had heard him say so. But what about the other son, the older son? What about him? The man had left Cody, too, and the thing Cody could never quite figure out was this: What, exactly, was wrong with him?

It was this question that stoked the coals of his anger, even when his past seemed forever behind him. No, Cody didn't ride bulls because he loved the rush. The rush was there, and it was real enough. Cody rode because battling a two-thousand-pound bull for eight seconds was the only way to live with the rage.

And as Cody Gunner moved into the public limelight, as he became the talk of the Pro Rodeo Tour, the invincible, undefeatable cowboy, it was that part he kept a secret. The fact that he didn't ride for the love of the sport; he rode because he had to.

Chapter Three

Ali Daniels sat in her trailer, not far from her mother, and stared out the window.

"This is my year." She gripped the arms of the swivel chair, her eyes unblinking.

"Yes." Her mom stood. "I can feel it." She opened a cupboard next to the miniature sink and pulled out a bulky vest. "Here." She handed it over. "Let's go, Ali. It's time."

A slow breath eased across Ali's lips. "Okay." She took the vest, slipped one arm through, then the other, and zipped it. A few more snaps and she was ready. She looked out again and saw a group of bundled-up cowboys making their way across the snow-covered parking lot toward Stadium Arena. They laughed, listening to the shortest one in the group, hanging on to whatever story he was telling. Not far back, three couples followed, headed the same way.

This was Denver in late January, the

season opener; festivities at the National Western Stock Show and Rodeo would start early and end late. Ali didn't mind missing the hoopla, as long as she was ready for her ride. The ride was all that counted.

She sat at the edge of her chair and kept her eyes on the people; so many people. Good for them for coming out, for cheering on the deserving professional rodeo riders and wranglers. But Ali didn't need them. She would've competed in an empty arena.

Anything to fly across the dirt, power and grace, an extension of the horse she'd spent years training. Sometimes she wasn't sure which of them loved the ride more, she or the muscled palomino horse she'd raised from birth.

"Ali?" Her mother touched her shoulder. "You okay?"

"Yeah." Her answer was quick. The walls of her chest ached, tighter than usual. Every breath was difficult, intentional, but what else could she say? How she felt wasn't a part of the equation; it never had been. "I'm fine."

"All right." She hesitated. "I'll get ready."

Familiar thoughts swirled about in Ali's heart.

Her popularity was building, not only because she was winning rodeos. She was a mystery, someone they'd dubbed beautiful and unreachable. She leaned forward and winced; the vest was tighter than usual. Yes, the public, the media, all of them held her up and examined her in the limelight. But there was very little she let them see.

She kept to herself, in her trailer with her mother or in a quiet corner of the locker room just long enough to change into her riding clothes. Friendships would be nice, but the less time she spent in the arena the better. She arrived in the tunnel minutes before each ride, and after the event she gathered her things and gave her horse a quick cooldown. Then she changed and headed back outside. The other barrel racers thought her distant, haughty, too good for them.

That wasn't it, but she couldn't explain herself. Not without giving away her secret, not without solving the mystery.

Her routine, her last-minute entry and quick exit from the arena, meant no time for cowboys, either. Just about all the single rodeo men and a few of the married ones had tried to hit on her in the past two years. Once in a while she would catch a smile or a glance from a cowboy who seemed nice enough. But there was no point, nothing she could offer in return.

Not when she was singly focused on two goals: staying healthy and being the best barrel racer in the world.

But the thing that really set her apart was something no one on the tour would ever know about. At least not while she was still competing. People wouldn't understand; they'd ask questions and make pronouncements about the risks and dangers. Before long the story would be out, and everyone would stop seeing her as the most promising barrel racer in rodeo.

Instead, they'd see her for her battles.

That would never happen; Ali was determined. Pro Rodeo would never know about her battles, her secret. They would never find out that she did something no other barrel racer did:

She held her breath when she rode.

From the tunnel around each of the three barrels, and back, she didn't draw a bit of air. The hooves of her horse would keep time with her heartbeat as the seconds played out, one after another. By the time she hit the tunnel again, she was desperate for air, her lungs screaming for relief.

Small wonder that she regularly clocked

in at less than eighteen seconds. Whether she was riding at the arena back home or racing for the national championship, every bit of her strength — even the energy it took to breathe — was focused on the ride. The fact that Ali held her breath when she raced was something only her parents knew about. Given the circumstances, they agreed that not breathing during the ride was her best chance of remaining a competitor.

It would be their secret.

So after two full years on the tour, Ali Daniels remained a curiosity, a blue-eyed rider with a thick ponytail of pale blonde hair, black hat and jeans, blazing across the arena on a horse as fair as she was. Reporters would ask her questions after a win, but her answers were never more than a few words. The details of her life went unknown.

The way they would stay.

Ali drew a slow breath and adjusted the vest. It was never comfortable; especially just before a ride, when all she wanted was to break free, run outside, saddle up Ace, and ride like the wind around the outside of the arena.

She bit her lower lip. Patience. There

was no riding without patience.

The truth was, she shouldn't have been here at all — not her, and not Ace. Ace was a quarter horse so small at birth his owner was willing to give him away. Only Ali had seen the horse's potential, rearing him and coaxing him and hand-feeding him until he was as big and strong as any horse on the tour.

That alone was shocking, because Ali's parents never wanted anything to do with horses.

Ali and her younger sister, Anna, grew up on a cattle ranch in Colorado, where her father made the rounds on an ATV quad-runner. Horses were off-limits, too much dander and dust, too many allergens, too great the chance that Ali and Anna might get sick. Because of their allergies, the sisters took their lessons at home in rooms cleaned by air purifiers. They were taught to read and sew and play the piano. Outdoor time was kept to a minimum.

But in the evening, when their parents were busy, Ali and Anna sat by the bedroom window and dreamed of another life. Ali remembered one time more clearly than the others.

"You know what I wanna do?" Anna's eyes sparkled that evening. "I wanna race through the forever hay fields and play hide-and-seek out by the tallest pine trees, and jump on that palomino horse next door." Anna was eight that year; Ali nine. The idea seemed wild and outrageous and terribly exciting. "Wouldn't that be something?"

"Yes." Ali squinted at the world beyond their sterile confines. "One day we will, okay, Anna? One day."

But the chance never came.

One afternoon when Anna was ten, she caught a cold. Something must've blown into the house from the garden, their mother always guessed. The cold became bronchitis, quick and fast. An asthma attack sent her to the hospital, and by the next day she had a respiratory infection. Within forty-eight hours her fever raged out of control. Pneumonia set in and because of her situation, no doctor or antibiotic could do a thing to help her. All their attempts at safety, all the years spent watching life through a window, had done nothing to save Anna. Three days later she was gone.

Anna's death changed everything for Ali, and she made up her mind. She would not watch life from a window; she would live it to the fullest, doing everything Anna had dreamed of doing.

The memory dissolved and Ali adjusted her vest again. She tried to draw a deep breath, but it wouldn't come; not fully.

She still had a few hours before her ride, so remembering helped pass the time. The season opener always stirred up the past, bringing reminders of how fortunate she was, how hard she'd fought against the odds and how easily this season — or any season — could be her last.

The pretty horse next door had a foal, and the foal became Ali's closest friend. He was the color of caramel custard with a mane the same pale blonde as Ali's long hair. She named him Ace, and against the odds, against the doctor's warnings, she spent every spare moment with him and grew stronger for it. With the neighbor's help, she broke him and trained him and learned to fly across the fields behind her parents' home.

Eventually she discovered barrel racing, and her father built an arena and a barn, with a custom air-filtration system to reduce the allergens from damp hay and horse dander. Ali remembered once when her aunt and uncle asked how her parents could be a willing party to something that might shorten their daughter's life.

Ali never forgot her father's answer.

"Riding horses *is* Ali's life," he told them. "It's that simple."

So it was.

On Ace she not only had a purpose — to round the barrels faster than anyone had before — but she felt vibrant, all of life bursting within her. And that feeling defied any sense of reason, because doctors and medicine and statistics said she should be dying.

The mystery was this: Ali Daniels had cystic fibrosis.

Cystic fibrosis — with all its terrible limitations and its lifetime sentence of having her back pounded two hours each day so she could cough up the thick secretions that would otherwise choke her. CF, the doctors called it, the same condition Anna had been born with. The disease in which every cold could go into pneumonia; and every bout of pneumonia could mean death.

Ali's parents never told her the prognosis for people with cystic fibrosis. She found it for herself — on the Internet. Patients with CF usually died as young adults, and though the life expectancy had risen, the outcome was certain.

One day, not too far off, the disease would kill her.

Ali adjusted her position again. The vest

was tight against her ribs, tight and uncomfortable. It wasn't for protection, the way the bull riders' vests were, though hers was customized to look like theirs. Rather, it was a compression vest. Powered by electricity, the vest had a series of air chambers, which rhythmically compressed Ali's lungs. The vest did mechanically what used to be done only by Ali's parents pounding on her chest and back.

One way or another, her lungs had to be cleared.

She leaned forward and let the vest work its magic. Ten more minutes and she'd be done. A series of coughs came over her, productive coughs. The type that kept her healthy. When she was finished, she closed her eyes and remembered again.

Her first rodeo came before her fourteenth birthday, the first time she and Ace tore around the barrels for a winning time. Three years later she hit the Pro Rodeo Tour, and she'd been hard to beat ever since.

Same as Cody Gunner.

The two of them were alike, both quiet, distant. Mysterious.

Ali was no longer amazed at how the crowd responded to Cody, how whole sections of women in the stands would wave their arms and chant his name when Cody received another saddle or a buckle. The sight of a six-foot-two bull rider with short dark hair, unrelenting blue eyes, and a confidence bigger than the arena left them collectively breathless.

Ali wasn't blind; the attraction was there for her, too. But that was as far as it went. As far as it would ever go. She'd shared the winner's circle with Cody too many times to count, and still they'd never said more than a polite hello to each other. Other cowboys would tip their hats or smile in her direction. Several made attempts at conversation.

Only Cody Gunner never tried, and that suited Ali fine. Cody was an island, a loner — just like her. He didn't flirt with the barrel racers or grin at the cowgirls who hung out near the stock pens; he didn't tend to the throng of female fans who waited for him after every rodeo.

The longer she rode the tour with him, the more Ali thought she understood him. The fact that he kept his distance didn't mean he was unkind, any more than she was unkind for keeping hers. On occasion, when their eyes met, Ali thought she saw a glimpse of something familiar in Cody's soul. A respect, maybe. A sameness. Whatever drove Cody Gunner to ride bulls for a living, Ali guessed it wasn't far off from what drove her. A passion born of something intensely private.

So while she didn't get weak at the knees in his presence, she quietly admired his independence, the way he didn't need people or trappings or success, but just the bull. Just the ride. He had placed second last year, just as she had.

This year — for one more season at least — they'd share the tour and the limelight with a single goal: a national championship. There was talk that Cody then might leave the tour, join Tuff Hedeman's upstart Professional Bull Riders circuit where the stock was more rank, the purses potentially bigger. If Cody was going to leave, this could be the last year they'd tour together.

Not that it mattered. That cold January day, the beginning of her third season in the PRCA, Ali Daniels had more important details to mull over than whether this was Cody's last season with the Pro Rodeo Tour. This was her year, the year she would stay healthy and strong and break record after record on her quest for the championship.

Ali and Ace, making history.

Her heart had room for nothing else.

Chapter Four

The season was three weeks old, and Cody Gunner was riding better than ever. The tour was in San Antonio, and his draw that night was a good one — a bull named Monster Mash, ridden just once in twenty-two attempts. A rider who could stay the course was guaranteed a score in the high eighties. Make it pretty and anything was possible.

Cody didn't worry about the judges. Scores didn't matter nearly as much as the eight seconds. If he got bucked off, Cody's anger would swell and grow, desperate for release. But if he stayed on for eight, he could beat the demons that battled him — if just for the night. There was the practical side, too. Winning meant enough money to keep playing the game.

Cody hung his rope in his locker, shoved his gear bag inside, and headed down the tunnel. Like most of the winter events, this one was at an indoor arena — the Joe and Harry Freeman Coliseum. It was his fifth season in the PRCA, so Cody knew his way around most of the venues. He tucked his shirt in as he walked, making sure the buttons lined up with his belt buckle.

Before he could stretch, before he could focus on the ride, he needed to know where he was in the lineup. He came into the clearing and turned right toward the information table, the place where the judges sat in a row, their paperwork spread out in front of them.

That's when something caught his attention.

A few feet away, leaning against the wall, was a fellow bull rider, a Brazilian who had taken first place from him three times the year before. Next to the cowboy was an older man with the same eyes, same cheekbones. The rider's father, Cody figured. He'd seen the two of them together before, in a handful of cities.

Cody watched them, watched the way the older man put his hand on the bull rider's shoulder, whispering something that made the cowboy smile. Probably some bit of encouragement or advice, something only a father could bring his son in the hour before a bull ride.

That was the way his own father had been with him before he walked out, wasn't it? Kind and compassionate, there with words of encouragement when Cody was up at bat in Little League or working on a school project?

Cody clenched his fists and turned from the scene. A young woman at the information table smiled at him.

"Cody Gunner, what can I do for you?"

Images of the Brazilian cowboy and his father burned in his mind. Cody focused on the woman. "Where am I in the order?"

The woman checked a list, grabbed a scrap of paper, and scribbled something. "Here." She handed it to him. "Good luck tonight."

Cody took the slip, nodded at her, and headed back down the tunnel. Halfway to the locker room he opened the paper. The woman had written that he rode second to last that night. At the bottom she'd scribbled her phone number.

He ripped the paper in half and went to his locker. It was time to stretch, even if his ride wasn't until the end. But he couldn't focus yet, couldn't let go of the picture in his head, the one of the rider and his dad.

What would it be like to ride bulls with his dad around, to get a dose of wisdom and confidence from his father before every ride? Cody opened his locker, pulled

61

out his worn deerskin riding glove, and slammed the door shut. He dropped to the bench, hung his head, and closed his eyes.

Of course the thought would haunt him today. There was no way around it, not after his mother's call that morning. She knew better than to call him the day of a ride, but she did it anyway. The news had made Cody sick to his stomach, unable to force down more than a piece of toast and an apple all day. Her call played in his mind again.

"He found us." Her voice was nervous, mixed with fresh hope.

"Who?" Cody had still been in bed, the hotel sheets a mess from the night before. He blinked back a hard night's sleep and tried to focus. He was alone, though he hadn't been a few hours earlier. What was his mother talking about, someone finding them? Had Carl Joseph wandered off? "Tell me later; I'm tired."

"Cody, you need to hear this." His mother's voice grew stronger, happier. "Your father found us, Cody. He called a few minutes ago; he wants to see you and Carl Joseph."

Cody had sat straight up in bed. His heart pounded hard, sending shock waves through his chest and throat and temples.

It wasn't possible. "My *father* called? After thirteen years he looks us up and you sound happy about it?"

Silence stood between them for a moment.

"He's sorry, Cody. Life hasn't been easy for him, either." She hesitated. "We had a long talk; he wants to see you."

Her words hit him like a load of buckshot, ripping at the places in his heart that still cared, still ached for his father no matter how much he told himself otherwise. A sound came from him, part laugh, part moan. Was she serious? How could she consider letting him back into their lives after what he'd done?

Cody leaned over his knees, the sheets loose around his waist. "I don't have a father."

"Cody, that's not how you feel, and —"

"I won't see him." His tone was sharp. "I need to go." He slammed down the phone, flopped back onto the pillow, and stared at the ceiling. The nausea hit him then. How dare he walk back into their lives now? How could he complain about his own life being hard when the whole mess was his fault?

Cody pressed his fists into his stomach and forced himself out of bed. What was the problem, anyway? He'd told her the truth; he didn't have a father.

But the conversation marred the entire day.

Normally the afternoon of a ride was marked by quiet preparation and nervous anticipation. In this case, he had both a hangover and his mother's phone call to shake off. The buildup felt flat, and all day he fought a headache.

Voices sounded outside the locker room door, and Cody hunkered down on the bench, his eyes still closed. The other cowboys would guess he was lost in concentration, readying himself for the ride. They'd leave him alone.

He pictured his father — however he must look with thirteen more years on him. Mike Gunner had played the field for more than a decade, shirked every ounce of family responsibility, and now — maybe because his son was a famous bull rider — he wanted back into their lives.

Worse, his mother was entertaining the possibility.

Adrenaline mixed with fury and ran hot through Cody's veins. He wanted to put his fist through the locker door, but he held back. *Save it for the bull, Gunner. Save it for the bull.* His eyes flew open. He stood, grabbed his rope, and headed down the tunnel.

The barrel racers were competing. He climbed a fence so he could stretch and watch at the same time. Over the loud-speaker the announcer was introducing the next ride.

"Ali Daniels is up, riding her longtime horse, Ace. Ali's on a streak of top-three finishes this season, and looking for the win here tonight. Anything less than fourteen-point-five seconds should do it, ladies and gentlemen."

He droned on about Ali's statistics, her intrigue and mystery.

Cody spread his legs wide until he felt the stretch along the inside of his thighs. Ali Daniels didn't need an introduction. Next to him, she was the most well-known competitor on the tour. Beautiful, strange, and mysterious. She rode with a reckless abandon that Cody understood innately, an abandon he admired.

From the first time he saw her compete, Cody wanted to go to her, wanted to be with her and ride with her and know every-thing about her. She was quiet and reclu-sive, confident and masterful in her talent. For all the girls who gave him no resis-tance, Ali was the ultimate challenge.

But he didn't allow those feelings to be anything more than fleeting. His success on the tour depended on his anger. He was twenty-one, too young to fall for a girl. Not even a girl like Ali Daniels. And so he ignored her at every rodeo — except when she competed.

Cody leaned to the right, focusing the stretch on that leg. Just then, Ali tore out of the tunnel, her head close to her horse's mane. She wasn't hard-looking like some of the barrel racers. Black hat and black jeans, a starched white shirt, her light blonde ponytail flying behind her, eyes intent on making the turn. Tight around the first barrel, then she blazed across the arena and around the second.

The crowd was already on its feet.

Every time Ali rode, there was the possibility of her setting a new record. That night was no exception. She rounded the third barrel and leaned forward. She and her horse blazed across the barrier at 14.35 seconds.

"Ladies and gentlemen, we have a new arena record! Ali Daniels shaved two-tenths of a second off the previous fastest time for barrels in this arena. She's sitting pretty safe for first place. Let's show her our appreciation."

Again the crowd cheered.

Cody wanted to peer into the tunnel, watch her pull up and dismount the way other cowboys watched Ali Daniels. But he wouldn't. Times like this he was glad he'd kept his distance. He didn't need any distractions.

He shifted his weight to the left leg, feeling the stretch stronger than before. Forty minutes passed, while the anger he harbored rose and grew within him. Forty minutes of picturing Carl Joseph's face as their mother explained the obvious — their father was gone. Forty minutes of hating him for walking out, for not making it clear to Cody what he'd ever done wrong, how he might've been responsible for making his daddy leave.

Forty minutes when Ali Daniels was just another rider on the tour, when his mother and even his brother might as well have been a million miles away, when nothing mattered in life except the battle, the damage he was about to do to a bull named Monster Mash.

"You got yourself the best draw of the night, Gunner." One of the cowboys slapped his back and took a step toward the chute next to Cody's. "You ready?"

"Ready."

"Let's get 'em." The cowboy nodded at the spectators. "It's a good crowd tonight; they deserve a show."

"Nothin' but eight."

The bull riders were lined up by then, gathered near the chute of whichever cowboy was next out. One at a time the riders flew into the arena, half of them making the eight seconds, the other half bucked off. Cody cheered them on, because that's what cowboys did. They pulled for one another. Bull riding never pitted a cowboy against his fellow rider. The contest was against the bull, only the bull.

But even as he cheered, his heart was back on a street corner the summer of his eighth year, watching for that yellow cab.

Cody zipped up his protective vest and spread his legs. Stretching was crucial; he'd been loosening up for an hour already. He bent at the waist, nose to his right knee, two, three, four, five. A little farther, and he switched sides, nose to his left knee, two, three, four, five. A shift to the center, straight back, palms to the ground, two, three, four . . . The whole time he kept his eyes on the bull.

An announcer was introducing the matchup.

"Monster Mash is a Texas Brahma bull, genetically engineered by the best in the business. Wicked horns, and a twist — about to keep a cowboy guessing."

The other announcer broke in. "Now remember, this is a bull that hasn't been rode ever. Not once. A killer beast with an average score of forty-eight-nine. Twenty-three cowboys on; twenty-three off."

"And Cody Gunner wants to change all that."

Cody tuned it out.

He felt himself slipping into the zone, the place where his little-boy disappointment, his unchecked rage and pent-up hatred, could be released. If only for eight seconds.

Finally it was his turn.

He pressed his cowboy hat onto his head, low over his brow, ran a few steps in place, and climbed the gate. One leg over the top of the chute, then the other. A push and he braced himself with his hands until he was straddled above the bull. Monster Mash was an ugly beast, mottled gray with uneven coloring and evil black eyes. His horns weren't much threat, but the hump on his back had knocked out a cowboy or two. Cody knew this, but he didn't think about it, didn't think about the bull's tendencies or any of the things most riders thought about.

All that mattered was this: The bull wanted to kill him.

Cody saw it in the way those dead eyes watched him, anxious, waiting. The bull had an innate sense, an ability to spot the cowboy, sniff out the next sacrificial victim. The animal shouldered the gates and pawed at the ground. Those awful eyes never let up, never blinked.

If there'd been a way through the bars, the bull would've found it.

Van Halen's "Jump" pounded out a rhythm that grew and built and filled each of the fifteen thousand fans with a frenzied anticipation. Bull riding was the last event, the biggest draw. Rodeo fans loved it. Loved the energy and intensity and possibility of horrific wrecks, the idea of mere mortals going head-to-head with an untamable beast.

"That's right," Cody glared at the animal, "go ahead and try it."

The bull jerked his head, shark-like eyes rolling back into his skull. Cody could picture it, knew what would happen the instant they opened the gate. The bull would become two thousand pounds of snorting, sweating muscle, writhing and twisting and flying through the hot summer night driven by one desire: Kill the cowboy.

The bull rider didn't need the announcers to tell him; he knew the score. Monster Mash couldn't be ridden, wouldn't let a cowboy sit on his back four seconds, let alone eight. Five guys stood on the outside of the gate, two of them holding tight to Cody's jacket, ready to pull him out if the bull went psycho. But Cody was ready. He lowered himself a foot, not quite touching the animal, his feet still on the steel rungs.

"Yeah, you want me." Cody gritted his teeth. The hatred was growing, filling him with a burning intensity, a seething red-hot rage. Everything but the bull faded from view, the bull and the profile of a face.

His father's face.

How could he walk out on us?

The hatred bubbled within him, mingled with liquid intensity and spilled into his icy veins, pumped through his ready limbs.

"Let's go, Gunner." A cowboy on the gate grabbed his arm and slapped his back.

It was time.

He lowered himself onto the bull, just down from the animal's shoulder blades. The beast's muscles trembled, furious, his hide hot and sweaty and loose over his bony spine. Monster Mash was famous for his damage in the chute, and today was no exception. The animal shifted all his weight sideways and Cody bit into his mouth guard.

He smacked the bull's shoulder. Fiery pain shot through his knee, the same knee he'd had pinned in the chutes six times this season. He couldn't leave the chute until he had his hand wrapped; couldn't wrap the hand until the bull let up, moved to the center, and freed his leg. Another whack and another. Fire shot up through his thigh. The deeper the pain, the more intense his hatred.

He was just a little boy, eight years old, full of laughter and love and kindness and goodness, and his little brother . . .

His little brother.

The rage tripled.

He shoved the bull's head. "Get outta there!" The animal moved three inches to the side and Cody jerked free. He shoved his right hand through the rope, palm up. Someone handed him the lead and he wrapped it hard, yanked it tight.

Cody wasn't sure if Monster Mash would spin to the outside or buck first. Films were available on every bull, and most riders memorized that sort of detail.

Not Cody. He wanted his bulls unpredictable, because fury and hatred and rage were unpredictable.

The bull rattled the chute again, jerking his head back and snorting, spraying the legs of the two closest guys, sounding like the beast he was, hating the cowboy. Cody slid forward to his tied-down hand, checked to make sure his knees weren't trapped. He locked his eyes on the animal's neck and gave the signal — a quick nod. A click of the latch, and the gate flew open.

"Go, Gunner!" another cowboy yelled.

He was one second into the ride when Monster Mash threw himself into a convulsion, all four hooves off the ground, twisting and snorting, kicking up dirt and dung in all directions. One-point-five seconds . . . two . . . two-point-five. The bull crashed down on his front feet, and already the animal's body was contorting in another direction, frantic to get the cowboy off his back. Cody kept his seat centered within a fraction of an inch, his legs tight around the bull.

Every late night wondering where his father was, why he hadn't called. Every birthday and Christmas and summer vacation without a gift or a card or even a call.

All of that hatred poured from him, releasing the rage that would otherwise strangle him.

Monster Mash was off the ground again, flying in a circle, kicking his backside up into the air, but Cody wasn't going anywhere. He leaned back, staying with the ride, holding center. A buzzer sounded and suddenly it was over.

With a flick of his wrist to release his riding hand, he kicked his feet over the side of the bull. But something was wrong. His hand was hung up, and with the animal's next arch of his back, Cody flopped like a rag doll alongside the bull's belly.

This had happened before; Cody didn't panic. No matter what the bull did to him now, he was the winner. He'd already won the battle. From both sides he felt the bull-fighters rush in, one of them grabbing at the end of the rope, trying to free his hand. The other waving something to distract the bull. The men might be dressed like clowns but they were willing to sacrifice their own bodies to keep a cowboy from danger. Cody was still caught up, still trying to free his hand, his body still being jerked along the side of the bull.

That's when he heard it.

A snap in his riding hand. At the same

time, Monster Mash whipped his head back at him. The hump on his back caught Cody square in the jaw and that was all he remembered. When he woke up, he was lying on a bench with the rodeo doctor staring at him.

"Cody . . ." The man was in his mid-thirties, the first one on the scene of any wreck on the Pro Rodeo Tour. "Can you hear me? Cody?"

"What?" His head hurt, but his heart and soul reveled in the release. He'd stayed the course, ridden Monster Mash for eight, and nothing could change the way that felt. He massaged his fingers into the sides of his head. "What was my score?"

The doctor chuckled. "On the knockout or the ride?"

Cody gave his head a slight shake. "Forget the knockout. I'm fine."

"You got an eighty-nine." The doctor shone a small flashlight into his eyes. "How're you feeling?"

"Better." Cody ran his tongue over his lower lip. "Eighty-nine?"

"Yes." The doctor frowned. "Lift your hand."

Cody tried to move it, and that's when he understood the doctor's frown. He winced, and supported it with his left hand. "It's just sprained."

"X-rays will tell."

Half an hour later, Cody had his bags packed for a two-week visit to his mother's house. A small bone in his hand was fractured, and he had a mild concussion. The doctor ordered two weeks off the bulls — minimum. Cody was given a splint for his hand and instructions to lay low.

He was on his way out of the training room when he spotted Ali Daniels.

Every other time they'd passed each other — for two years straight — they barely looked up. Today, though, Ali paused.

"Want some advice?" She took another step toward him, a bridle flung over one shoulder.

Too stunned to answer, Cody stopped and sized her up. She was five-foot-six, maybe five-seven, and up close her eyes shone like summer lake water. He leaned against the nearest wall and grinned at her. "Okay."

"If you can stay on eight, stay on nine." She smiled and started walking again. "At least until your hand's free."

She was gone before he could recover, before even a single comeback formed on his tongue. Was she kidding? Did she think she had information that might help Cody Gunner ride bulls better? And why did she talk to him now, after so many events where they had never connected?

Cody had no answers. Maybe it was a delusion; concussions could do that to a person. He watched her leave and let the comment pass. He didn't have time for Ali Daniels or any of the other girls who would be waiting for him outside the arena. He had something far bigger ahead of him — two weeks to talk sense into his mother. That way, the next time his father called she could do what she should've done the day before.

Hang up on him.

Chapter Five

Mary Gunner loved having her older son home.

Out on the road, riding a slate of bulls every weekend, meant that bad news was always just around the corner. Mary knew the sport well enough to know the possibilities, and they terrified her. So when Cody showed up with his hand in a splint needing two weeks of rest, she was grateful.

Quietly grateful.

Cody wouldn't have it any other way. His anger at her hadn't dimmed from the days after Mike left. Never mind that his blaming her made no sense. The moment he entered the house he looked around, his expression tense.

"Where is he?"

Mary held his eyes for a moment, then she turned toward the stairs and cupped her mouth. "Carl Joseph! Your brother's home."

The sound of pounding footsteps came

in response. "Brother!" the voice bellowed from an upper room.

"I'm down here, buddy!" Cody went to the foot of the stairs and looked up.

"Coming, brother!" Carl Joseph was fifteen now, still attending a special-education program where they were teaching him menial tasks. Most days Mary was grateful for Carl Joseph's Down syndrome. It meant that at least one son would always love her. One son would keep her company the way Cody never did.

Carl Joseph barreled down the stairs and gave Cody a long bear hug. When he pulled back, his eyes danced. "How's the bulls, brother?"

"Well . . ." Cody held up the hand that bore the cast. "Not so good this weekend."

"Ooooh!" He touched Cody's cast and shook his head. "You be careful, brother. You be careful."

Cody chuckled. "I will." He put his arm around Carl Joseph's neck and led his brother into the next room.

For two weeks straight the two were inseparable. They played checkers and backgammon and watched videotapes of bull riding on TV. The morning after Cody left, Carl Joseph found Mary reading a book in the living room.

"Mom, I have a question." He came a few steps closer.

Mary held her hand out to him. "What, honey?"

"How come Cody doesn't like you?" Carl Joseph cocked his head, his mouth open. "How come, Mom?"

The question tore at Mary's heart, but it was an honest one, proof that Cody's bad attitude wasn't only her imagination. She cleared her throat, searching for a way to explain the situation. She couldn't mention Mike. Carl Joseph didn't remember his father, and if Mike wanted back into their lives — the way he said he did — she didn't want to taint Carl Joseph's image of him.

"Cody loves me." Mary bit her lip, fighting tears. "But sometimes his heart doesn't work the same as yours."

"Brother's heart doesn't work right?" Carl Joseph thought about that for a minute. "You know what I hope?"

Mary slid to the edge of her seat, her eyes damp. The compassion in Carl Joseph was every bit as intense as the hatred in Cody. "What, honey?"

"I hope that Cody's heart will get better, just like his hand."

Mary hugged her younger son. "So do I,

honey." He couldn't know that's what she'd hoped and prayed for years, what she prayed for even now — that one day Cody would meet someone who would teach him more than horses and rodeos and bull riding. Someone who might teach Cody the most important lesson of all.

How to love.

Cody was back on the tour, riding as if he'd never hurt his hand at all. Yes, he was using a lot of tape, wrapping his hand and forearm tighter than before. But a little pain was nothing. It made the battle that much more intense. Fighting not just the bull, but pain and injuries, too.

He was in second place in the standings, ten points below first despite two missed weekends. Regaining the lead was as sure as morning. His nighttime hours were different, too, fewer beers and women, cleaner, the way they always were after a few weeks with Carl Joseph.

His mother called twice in the next few weeks.

"Your father's been by," she told him during the first phone call. "Carl Joseph likes him. They played football in the backyard."

Football? The idea made Cody's gut

ache. Mike Gunner, big former NFL player, loses thirteen years of his kids' lives and then shows up and tosses a ball around? Like nothing ever happened?

"He's asking about you, Cody," she told him the next time. "He wants to watch you ride."

"Tell him no." Cody was in the locker room. He dropped to the bench and gripped the edge of it, his voice low so the other cowboys passing in and out wouldn't hear him. In the background Lynyrd Skynyrd was singing "Sweet Home Alabama" over the arena speakers.

"I won't do that, Cody." His mother sounded impatient.

Cody pinched his eyes shut. What was the feeling tearing at him? Hatred, right? More anger and fury? But it didn't feel like only that. It felt like little-boy sadness, too. A sadness that didn't make sense because he'd banned it from his heart the day the yellow cab drove away.

"Cody, when can he see you?" His mother sounded tired, as if she knew his answer before he said it.

"Never." He pursed his lips. "I have nothing to say to him."

Whatever his mother wanted to accomplish by calling him, the end result was a good one. That weekend and the next, he took first and second, and now he had the lead heading into the final go-round in Houston at the Reliant Center. The barrel racing was under way, and Cody took his spot on the fence, stretching the insides of his legs and the muscles that lined his groin.

As always, he watched Ali's race. She was every bit as fast as usual, but this time something was wrong; her face was red and puffy. He looked around but no one along the fence looked worried, as if maybe he was the only one who saw that she was in trouble.

He was off the fence, jogging toward the tunnel before she crossed the barrier. He stepped into view just in time to see her hop down from her horse and lower her head between her knees.

She was coughing so hard she couldn't catch her breath. Cody stared for a minute. Was she sick? Was it asthma? Maybe she was choking. He grabbed a cup of water from a nearby cooler. With no one around, Cody wasn't sure what to do. He took tentative steps closer until she looked up.

"Ali?" He closed the distance between them and held out the cup.

She hacked again. "Thanks." She took it

and downed it in a single swig. A few more coughs and the redness in her face started to fade. She leaned against her horse, clearly exhausted from the struggle. "I'm okay. I . . . I guess I have a cold."

"I guess." He took a step back. "I've never heard anyone cough like that."

She folded her arms in front of her and stared at him, eyes wide. Then she nodded her chin toward the arena. "Your ride's coming up."

"Yeah." He tipped his hat to her. "Get better." He trotted off for the chutes, surprised by one thing.

Ali Daniels wasn't superhuman after all; he'd seen a vulnerable side of her. It was all he could do to shut her image out of his mind while he rode. The first bull that night tripped and fell to his knees, giving Cody a re-ride. He lasted eight on the second. His score wasn't great, but it was enough to win, and less than half an hour after her coughing episode, Ali Daniels stood next to him in the arena while they both accepted their championship buckles.

They were headed back down the tunnel when Cody fell in beside her. "Hey . . . wanna go out? Get something to eat?"

Ali hesitated. She met his eyes but only for a few seconds before staring straight ahead. "I can't; I have plans."

"Plans?" Cody allowed a smile into his voice. It wasn't that he doubted her, but she traveled with her mother, and the two of them were in her trailer before ten o'clock every night. What plans could she possibly have?

"Yes, Cody Gunner." She angled her face, teasing him. Her eyes didn't look quite right, maybe the cold she was fighting. "I have a hot date, okay?"

Cody wanted to laugh out loud, but he couldn't. He didn't know her well enough to assume she was kidding. Instead he shrugged and winked at her. "Suit yourself."

He held the door open for her and they headed into the night — her to her mother's trailer and whatever hot date she had that night, and Cody to the nearest bar to meet up with the other cowboys.

But it was another early night for him.

Dinner was good, the beer was flowing, and half a dozen girls made themselves available. But he wasn't interested. No matter what they looked like or how they presented themselves, or what they had to offer, Cody couldn't help but compare them to Ali Daniels.

And since they all fell short, he did the

right thing. When he turned the key of his hotel room that night he was by himself, except for the place in his memory filled with the blonde, blue-eyed barrel racer.

A girl whose level of mystery had doubled in a single conversation.

Chapter Six

The hot date was a private plane ride to Denver General Hospital.

Ali had been expecting the visit since the second week of the season, and it frustrated her. This was the year she didn't want to miss a single event, the year she planned to keep herself healthy so she wouldn't need any downtime in a hospital bed.

But her body had other ideas.

It was Monday night now, and her mother was in the chair beside her bed. Dr. Bryce Cleary was due any minute, the same doctor who had treated Ali since she began riding horses. The visit wasn't any surprise, really. Since early in the season, her coughing had been more intense, the spells closer together.

The lives of cystic fibrosis patients are directed by test results. Bacteria analysis, lung function, nutritional deficiencies, enzyme levels. All have to be closely monitored. When one or more of Ali's readings fell into their respective danger zones, it was time to see Dr. Cleary.

In the hospital she would be on constant oxygen and intravenous antibiotics. Her body would get the rest it needed, the infection she was fighting would clear up, and after a week she could get on with living. At least that's how it had always played out before.

Ali rolled onto her side and studied her mother. "You look worried."

"I'm not much for hospitals; you know that." She reached out and took Ali's hand.

"Me either."

They were quiet for a minute. Ali knew what her mother was thinking — the same thing she was thinking. Anna died in a room like this one, her body trying to find the way back to daylight. They both know cystic fibrosis patients weren't admitted to the hospital unless their situation was serious.

There were no guarantees, no certainties that this would be merely another tune-up, another pit stop between rodeo appearances.

Her mother leaned back in her chair. "After your win the other night" — their eyes met — "why was Cody Gunner talking to you?"

A smile lifted the corners of Ali's mouth before she could stop it. "He asked me out."

"Cody Gunner?" Her eyebrows lifted, creasing her forehead. She still held Ali's hand, but now she loosened her grip. "Why didn't you tell me?"

"I couldn't breathe; I guess I was distracted." Her smile softened. For a minute she could see Cody's face as he walked next to her. "It's okay, Mama. I'm not interested."

Her mother hesitated. A slow breath came from her. "You know I have hopes and dreams for you. That you'll live long enough to be loved, that when the time's right you'll meet someone. Someone who'll sweep you off your feet and take you away from horse dander and dusty arenas and damp hay." She looked at the ceiling. "But heaven forbid it be someone like Cody Gunner."

Ali laughed, and the effort brought on a wave of coughs. "Mama . . . I told you I wasn't interested." She gulped, catching her breath. "Wish for my health, but don't wish that I'll meet someone." She stroked her thumb along her mother's hand. "I am loved — by you and Daddy. I have the life I want — me and Ace, winning on the

89

rodeo tour, flying across arenas in every city on the schedule." She felt her expression soften. "That's all I need."

Her mother looked at her, a look that went straight to her soul. "Ali, before you die, I want you to be loved the way your father loves me. Loved by a man who would give anything for you." She paused. "Horses can't compare to a love like that."

Ali didn't respond. Her mother was wrong, of course. Horses were enough; they had always been enough. But there was no changing her mother's mind. They had this discussion at least once a month. Ali believed her mother was less interested in her meeting a man than she was in her leaving the rodeo tour.

She bit her lip. She'd already told her mother the way she felt about falling in love. She wouldn't do it. She'd dated once, the year before she joined the PRCA. After a series of colds and a hospital stay, the boy told her he couldn't handle her being sick. And he didn't even know about her cystic fibrosis.

The experience convinced her that dating was a waste of time. She didn't want to disappoint someone every time she got sick; and in the end, any relationship would end too soon. That was the way of life for a cystic fibrosis patient.

Riding Ace was enough; it was all she wanted. Her mother could dream twenty-four hours a day, but nothing would change Ali's determination. She would stay on the Pro Rodeo Tour until her body gave her no choice but to quit. Then she would live with her parents until the end. No sad good-byes other than the ones she would have with them and Ace.

There was a knock at the door and Dr. Cleary entered the room. "Hi." He had a manila file in his hand. "How're you feeling, Ali?"

"Better." She rolled onto her back and released her mother's hand. "My lungs are still full, though. I can feel them."

"Yes." The doctor came to the foot of her bed and looked at her. "Your numbers could be better. You've lost some weight, so I'm increasing your enzymes."

"That's what the nurse said." Ali managed a smile. The routine was the same every time. Eat more, take the enzymes, adjust the medication. She wanted him to get to the good part, the part where he told her how long until she could be released, until she could be back at her next rodeo.

"Is it worse than before?" Her mother's lips were pale, narrow and pinched. Her fear was palpable. She forced a tight smile. "You know Ali. She thinks these visits are tune-ups." She paused. "Is this one different?"

"Well . . . yes." The doctor opened the file and sorted through several sheets. He looked up and met Ali's eyes. "It's different because after two full days of treatment, her lungs aren't responding the way I'd like."

Ali's heart missed a beat. She had grown up around doctors and hospitals; nothing in the medical world frightened her. But what was Dr. Cleary saying? She propped herself up. "So increase the medicine, right? Is that what's next?"

The doctor closed the file and let his hands fall to his sides. "Ali, your lung tissue is losing elasticity. You've always known this was where you were headed."

Her mother lifted her chin, her back stiff. "So, what does that mean? She stays in the hospital longer?"

"We'll increase her medication and keep her for a week, like always." He pursed his lips. "The problem is, at this point, her lungs can't rebound as well. Every time her numbers get bad, she'll lose some of her lung capacity permanently. Some of the bacteria won't ever go away. That's where we're at."

Ali swallowed against the lump in her throat. The doctor was wrong; he had to be. Her lungs weren't worse than usual; the feeling was the same as always. "Isn't there anything . . . can't you give me something to bring them back all the way, like before?"

"Yes." The doctor's tone was gentle but stern. "I can give you an order, Ali. When you leave the hospital this time, go home and stay home. Sell your horse and take up piano again. You have to stay away from all irritants if you want to slow this thing."

Ali shook her head, her mind spinning. The doctor's order was out of the question. Impossible. She glanced at her mother. Was that relief in her eyes? Did she pay the doctor to come up with such a crazy suggestion? She leaned on her elbows and met the doctor's eyes straight on. "I'm in the middle of a season, Doctor. I'm not quitting."

The doctor clutched the file to his middle and looked at her, silent. Something in his expression told Ali he was being straight with her. Remorse fell into the mix of feelings burying her. She couldn't blame Dr. Cleary. The news wasn't easy for him either.

Finally he drew a slow breath and looked at them.

"Let me make it clearer." He opened the folder again. "The dust and molds and allergens at horse arenas have done permanent damage to your lungs. If you don't stop riding, you'll need a lung transplant in a year or less."

A lung transplant? Things were that bad?

Ali's heart raced and the mattress beneath her felt wobbly and off-balance. Cystic fibrosis patients didn't get lung transplants until their situations were dire. Unless . . . She held her breath, hopeful. Maybe things were different now, maybe a lung transplant would cure her. "Would that make me better?"

Her mother hung her head and shaded her eyes. This was the worst possible news; the news all of them had dreaded since Ali started riding horses.

The doctor took a step closer. "Nothing's changed." He patted Ali's hand. "A transplant buys you three years, maybe four. Less if you don't take care of yourself."

"Doctor . . ." Her mother lifted her head. Tears pooled in her eyes. "Are you saying if Ali doesn't stop riding she *could* need a transplant, or she *will* need one?"

The doctor brought his lips together and exhaled in a way that filled his cheeks. He gave a sharp sideways shake of his head. "Anything could happen, Mrs. Daniels. There's a chance she could return to riding and not see things get worse for more than a year. Two or three years even. But eventually it'll catch her. I'm completely certain of that."

Ali was trembling. What were all the tubes attached to her, anyway? She wanted to rip them from her arms and run from the room, from the awful news. But something the doctor said caught her attention. "So you could be wrong? About needing it within the year?"

"You can hear what you want to hear." The doctor's expression was soft, sympathetic, but he sounded defeated. "I'm advising you to stop riding — the sooner, the better."

Ali stared at him. Then she let her head fall back against the pillow. "I won't stop." She closed her eyes. "Please, do everything you can to make me better. I'll finish this season, and then I'll decide."

The doctor knew not to argue. He'd recommended against horses since she was eleven. "Very well." He took a few steps back. "I'd like to run tests on your parents; see if they'd be a match. We're doing transplants with live donors these days, but it

95

takes two people to pull it off."

"Live donors?" Her mother looked hopeful, and Ali's heart hurt for her.

"It's a serious ordeal, Mrs. Daniels. One donor gives the lower right lobe, the other gives the lower left. Anyone who donates a lobe will experience a permanent loss in lung function."

"That wouldn't be a problem." She nodded. "We'd like to be tested right away."

With that, the doctor was gone. Ali wanted to scream and cry and bury her head in the pillow. She didn't want her parents going through something that drastic, a difficult surgery and the loss of lung function. Not when it had always been her decision to keep riding, to put her health at risk.

She opened her eyes and looked at her mother. "I'm sorry, Mom." She reached out and took her hand again. The doctor could check all he wanted; she wouldn't take a lung from either of her parents. It wasn't their fault she was sick. It was her own. Her determination to keep riding.

"Ali" — her mother's eyes pleaded with her — "You're the best in rodeo. Isn't that enough?"

"I haven't won a national championship,

Mama. Ace and I can do it. It might still happen this season." Her lungs hurt from the emotion building within her. "I can't stop riding; you know that."

Instead of yelling at her or demanding she stop, her mother dabbed at her eyes and stared at her folded hands. "I don't know how we'll tell your father."

Ali felt the victory all the way to her soul. "He'll understand."

She looked up and their eyes held. "I understand, too. I just want to keep you around a little longer."

"I know. Thanks, Mama."

She was released from the hospital a week later with a stronger arsenal of medicines and inhalers and strict orders to use her vest two to three times a day. Especially at rodeos.

The next week while she recuperated at home, watching old movies with her father and helping her mother in the kitchen, Cody Gunner's name never came up.

Except in Ali's mind.

She'd told her mother the truth; she wasn't interested. Not in Cody or anyone else. Despite her mother's prayers to the contrary, she would not get involved with a man; not when she had so little time, when her sport demanded every spare moment.

Still, her first night out of the hospital, when her parents had turned in and sleep wouldn't come, when the prospect of getting off Ace for good or being relegated to a lung transplant left her too frightened to close her eyes, she found comfort in one thing alone. The memory of Cody Gunner leaving his place on the fence to bring her a cup of water. The sound of his voice, the feel of his body a foot from hers in the tunnel, the guarded kindness in his voice as he asked her out.

By morning, she shook off the crazy thoughts and promised to never entertain them again. Cody Gunner? Any thought of him was ridiculous, unwanted. She didn't care a bit for the guy. He was a player, a renegade who needed no one. It was one thing to ride horses against her doctor's orders. But to have feelings for Cody Gunner?

Even she wasn't that crazy.

Chapter Seven

Cody hated himself for worrying, but he couldn't help it.

For two straight events, Ali Daniels hadn't shown up and that could only mean one thing. Her cold was worse than he'd thought. Maybe it wasn't a cold, but pneumonia. Maybe she was in the hospital.

Thoughts of her distracted him, and he rode below what he was capable of at both events, taking a fourth place and a no-score. The third weekend, he spotted her trailer and felt himself relax. Whatever the problem, she must have recovered.

He saw her that Saturday morning, several hours before the spectators were scheduled to arrive. She was riding her horse in the field behind the arena, tearing up one way, circling imaginary barrels, and then racing like the wind back toward the edge of the parking lot.

Cody loved horses, but he didn't own one. Most of the time he flew to events and stayed in hotels. Ali and the other competitors who relied on their horses traveled in motor homes, pulling horse trailers. He wandered toward the stock area and borrowed a horse from one of the steer wrestlers. In an easy motion, he swung himself into the saddle and galloped out to the field toward Ali.

She looked healthy and tanned; her cheeks clear of the puffy redness.

He pulled up near her. She turned two tight circles, then stopped and faced him. He held her gaze. "You've been gone."

"Yes." Without tugging on the reins, the animal leaned his head back, and she rested against his neck. She was breathless from the workout. "Did you get hung up while I was away?"

A strange feeling worked its way through Cody's gut, a feeling he couldn't quite identify. He allowed the hint of a smile. "I would've." He leaned forward, his hands covering the saddle horn. "But I got the best advice."

"Really?" Her expression was light, easy.

"Really." He danced his horse sideways a few steps. "Someone told me if I could stay on for eight, I could stay for nine. You know, use the extra second to untie my hand so I wouldn't get hung up."

"Well?" She shifted back in her saddle. "Did it work?"

"Like a charm." He lifted his hands so she could see them. "No more casts."

"Hmmm." She raised one eyebrow. "Imagine that." Her heels pressed against her horse's belly. And without further warning, she was off, flying down the field, clearly intent on finishing her workout.

Cody watched her, and the challenge was too great to pass up. He switched the reins from one side of the horse's neck to the other. "Yah!" And suddenly he was tearing up the field after her, mesmerized by her speed and ability. He didn't catch up with her until she reached the far side.

She brushed her hair off her face, her cheeks ruddy from the exertion. "Are you chasing me?"

He held the reins tight against his waist. With the sun on her face, exhilarated from the ride, she wasn't only beautiful. She was irresistible. He waited until he had his breath again. "Do you want me to?"

"No." A laugh came from her, one that sounded like the most delicate wind chimes. "There's no point."

"Why not?" His words were slow, the conversation unhurried. They were far enough from the arena that no one could see them, no one would wonder why Cody Gunner was talking to Ali Daniels.

"Because" — she smiled — "I don't want to be caught." She set her horse in motion again. "See ya."

There was laughter in her voice. She was kidding, of course. All girls wanted to be caught. But maybe Ali was different in this, too. He didn't ride after her. Instead he set out at a diagonal, back toward the stock pen. He returned the horse and headed to the hotel for breakfast.

It took him an hour to stop replaying their conversation in his head. He chided himself, hating the way she'd distracted him that morning. If she didn't want to be caught, fine. He wouldn't chase her.

He needed his focus, needed to stay angry, in touch with the rage. Nothing in his riding regimen had room for the strange feelings she stirred inside him. But after their encounter that morning, he couldn't get into a rhythm, couldn't find the way back to the pain that kept him centered on the back of a bull for eight violent seconds. He was bucked off an easy ride, a bull that had been ridden 70 percent of the time.

He was walking down the tunnel, disgusted, when he saw Ali sitting by herself outside the locker room. She was coughing, but she stopped when she saw him.

"Ready for more advice?" She stood and leaned against the wall.

Normally after a buck-off, he wouldn't talk to anyone. But his frustration had no staying power in her presence. He stopped and crossed his arms. "Let me guess, don't fall off, right?"

"No." She pushed the toe of her boot around in the dirt. A smile lifted her lips. "That would help, but you should anticipate more. The way you ride, it's all about reacting. You should balance that. Focus on the feel of the bull's shoulders and anticipate his next move. Anticipation first; then reaction." She lifted one shoulder and fell in alongside him. "Couldn't hurt."

He stopped just before the men's locker room door. "Thank you, Ali." His tone was dry, mildly sarcastic. He was still dusty from being bucked off the easiest bull at the rodeo. She couldn't expect him to be cheerful. "How did I get along without you?"

"That one" — she pushed the door of the women's locker room and grinned — "I can't help you with."

Cody waited outside the arena for her, but she never showed.

He was on his way back to the hotel when two bull riders and a half dozen scantily dressed girls met him in the parking lot. He hung with them for a few hours, but just before midnight — when one of the girls moved onto his lap — Cody called it a night.

As he fell asleep, he promised himself he wouldn't lose another go-round because of Ali Daniels. She wasn't interested, and neither was he. That was reason enough to put her out of his mind.

The next day he was getting ready for his ride when his heart dropped.

Not ten yards ahead of him stood his mother and his brother and a man who looked very much like his father. Cody glared at the man. Was it really him? Had he come without being invited? Cody wanted to walk up and punch him in the face, release on the man a fraction of the rage he felt when he climbed on a bull. But not in front of Carl Joseph. He was about to turn around when his mother spotted him.

"Wait, Cody." She wore jeans, and a red sweater he'd never seen before. She took light running steps toward him. "Don't leave."

He shook his head and took a step back,

but it was too late. Carl Joseph saw him. "Brother! Hi, brother!"

Cody stopped. He gritted his teeth and ordered his heart to kick into a normal beat. When his mother was inches from him, he leaned in, his voice strained. "Why'd you bring him?"

"He wanted to come." She wore sunglasses, but he could see the fear in her face. "You're his son, Cody. You need to talk to him."

Carl Joseph was loping up. "Brother! Guess what?"

"Hey, buddy." Cody couldn't let his brother know he was mad. "You gonna watch me ride tonight?"

"Yeah, and guess what?" He jumped a few times in place. "I met my dad. He's your dad, too!" Carl Joseph pointed at the man, still waiting ten yards back. "See, brother. That's him. That's our dad!"

The excitement in Carl Joseph's voice made Cody furious. The nerve of the man, coming back into their lives and getting Carl Joseph's hopes up. When he walked out the next time it would change the kid forever, just as it had changed Cody.

Carl Joseph tugged on his arm. "Come meet him, brother. He wants to talk to you."

A seething hatred consumed him. He shot another angry look at his mother. It took all his effort to keep his tone even. "Listen, buddy, I need to get ready for my ride. I'll talk to him later, okay?"

"Okay." Carl Joseph gave him a dramatic high five. "Have a good ride, brother!"

Without saying another word to his mom, without another glance at his father, he turned and headed fast in the opposite direction. That night — intently aware that somewhere in the stands his father was sitting next to Carl Joseph — the ride was easier than it had been in weeks. Cody rode out his rage, taking every bit of it out on the bull. In the process he kept a seat on a beast known for its violent wrecks.

Cody's score for the night was ninety-three — his highest of the season, and enough to put him in the championship round.

He stayed in the locker room until he was sure his family was gone. When he was ready to leave, he exited to the outdoors. There would be no partying for him that night; not when he had a decade of emotions to sort through. Before turning in, there was something he had to do. He made his way through the parking lot to Ali's trailer and gave a light knock on the door.

She wore jeans and a sweatshirt, and in the moonlight she looked impossibly beautiful. "Cody . . . what're you —"

"Ali." He tipped his hat, a grin tugging at his mouth. "Just wanted to thank you for the advice. My win tonight . . . it was all you."

With that he turned and headed for the hotel across the street. He was gone before she could respond.

Chapter Eight

Cody avoided Ali as much as possible.

They were midway through the season, and points were crucial if he wanted to take a lead into the summer. After seeing his father, he had no trouble focusing, no difficulty identifying the demons only bull riding could battle. He won three straight and by the first part of June there was no one close.

His mother still called, but he didn't mind. Every conversation about his father was fuel for the fire, another reason to attack the bull, to go the distance no matter how violent the ride. The guy was serious about coming back. He took a job coaching at a small college a mile from their house. The story was the same with every phone call. His father was desperately sorry, anxious for a second chance.

"The call of every Christian is to forgive," his mother told him one morning. "Please, Cody, give him a chance."

"That's funny." Cody wanted to laugh. "I thought the call of every Christian was to love." He tightened his grasp on the cell phone. "Remind him of that, why don't you."

His mother didn't miss a beat. "What would you know of love, Cody? You don't love anyone but Carl Joseph. No one else gets in."

"I don't need anyone else."

"You do, Cody. You'll waste your whole life fighting make-believe battles if you don't turn around and see the truth. We all love you, Cody. Carl Joseph and I, and even your father."

Cody was shaking by then. "Don't mention his name again or I'll hang up."

The battle raged.

Cody could only guess how the situation with his parents would turn out, but he was sure of this: He wouldn't go home again. Not until his father was out of the picture. The man had changed the course of his life, sent him chasing after death every weekend of the year. He should've been playing football for some college team by then, but instead he was crippled with rage.

A rage that was worse than ever, one even bull riding barely eased.

★ ★ ★

Ali could tell Cody was staying away.

He was winning, but he looked angry as he stormed around the arena, angry and distant. The two of them hadn't spoken to each other in weeks.

That was okay; Ali was fighting her own battles.

Despite an arsenal of stronger medications and inhalers, she was struggling during events. She could still hold her breath during the ride, but afterwards, when she grabbed that first bit of air, she would slip into a coughing spasm that sometimes lasted five minutes.

Other riders had begun to notice. Whereas they typically kept their distance, reacting to her aloofness, now a few of them expressed concern.

"You should see a doctor about that cough," an older rider told her the day before. "You sound like you have pneumonia."

If they only knew.

That day, Ali added a third session with the compression vest. The treatment helped, but a few hours later she finished her ride with one of her slowest times of the season, and afterwards she lapsed into a series of coughs that wouldn't let up.

She was doubled over near her horse when she felt his hand on her shoulder.

"Ali . . . here." This time Cody handed her a full water bottle. "Maybe you're allergic to dust."

"Maybe." Ali took a long drink. She had her own water, but it was twenty yards away, near the back of the tunnel. Another swig and she could feel her lungs relax, feel the air making its way into even the stubborn areas that were no longer soft and pliable. "I'm fine." She wiped her brow and met his eyes. "Thanks."

He studied her for a minute. "I have to go."

"Yep." She smiled. "My advice is still paying off."

Cody grinned and let his gaze fall to his boots. When he looked up, his eyes were more vulnerable than before. "Can I ask you something?"

"You just did." She lowered her chin, her eyes big. It felt fun to tease him.

"I'm serious, Ali." He looked over his shoulder at the arena. The last barrel racer was about to go. His ride was coming up.

"Okay." She took another drink from the bottle. She could breathe now; but she needed to get out of the tunnel. The dust there was almost as bad as it was on the barrel course. She squinted at him. "Ask."

"Why do you ride sick?"

The words skipped across the surface of her heart like a series of smooth stones. She met his gaze, unblinking. "Why do you ride angry?"

He mulled over her question and finally gave her a slow nod. "The answers are somewhere, aren't they?"

"Probably."

"Let's talk tonight." The teasing faded from his eyes. "Can we do that, Ali?"

The truck was circling the barrel course now; a handful of cowboys tossing the bins in the back, clearing things for the bull riders. Ali knew what her mother would think. Anyone but Cody Gunner . . . She looked at the arena. "You need to go."

"Tell me, Ali. We'll find someplace and talk for an hour. Nothing more."

Ali bit her lip. She needed to wear the vest for an hour before she could do anything. "Come by my trailer around eleven. Knock once on the door; I'll be waiting."

For the first time in weeks, the anger lifted entirely from Cody's face. "Me, too."

Ali rarely stayed in the arena long enough to watch the bull riders. If she wanted her lungs to bounce back from a race, she needed to get Ace out to the stock pens so she could breathe fresh air. Then, as soon as possible, she would return to the trailer and slip on the compression vest.

Her mother would already be there, waiting.

But that night, she wanted to watch Cody ride. So she took care of Ace and headed back down the tunnel toward the arena. Bull riders were crazy. Ali had always thought so. It was one thing to ride a horse around a pattern of barrels. But to sit on a bucking bull, to think for a minute it was possible to master two thousand pounds of muscled beast, that was crazy.

Crazy and dangerous.

One of the riders that night got hung up on a bull's horns. He was almost free when the bull jerked his head back and hit the rider's face square on. It wasn't as bloody as it could've been, but the rider was knocked out, cold.

The bullfighters rushed in and distracted the animal, saving the rider's life. When it was safe, a stretcher was brought out. Even the announcer — usually optimistic in the face of injuries, sounded concerned. Two riders later a cowboy was bucked off and landed on his head. He lay motionless for nearly a minute before giving a weak movement with first his hands, then his feet.

Two more riders and then it was Cody's turn.

The announcer was commenting on Cody's luck, how he always seemed to draw the rankest bulls. That was a good thing because half the rider's score came from the bull's ability to buck. The best stock could twist in more than one direction and keep their front and back feet off the ground at the same time, flying through the air.

Ali read the reports. Cody had a knack for drawing that type of bull at least once every rodeo. She watched him climb onto the bull, and that's when she saw it. She was right; he rode angry. From the moment he straddled the bull, his jaw was set, his eyes narrow. They showed his face on the big screen, and his expression was so colored with rage it made her take a step back.

The chute opened and Cody held on, focused and intent. The seconds ticked off, and Cody didn't give the bull a single centimeter's edge. He stayed perfectly centered, his left hand in the air no matter what the bull did to buck him off.

His ride brought him an eighty-six, good

enough for second place heading into the final go-round the next day. Ali hurried out of the arena, her stomach in knots. What was the feeling inside her? The strange fluttering of her heart when he survived the ride and pumped his fist in the air? Was it the oneness, the sameness Ali had recognized in him before?

Ali had no answers as she darted through the rows of trailers and RVs. When she reached theirs, her mother was outside waiting. "Where've you been?"

"Talking." Ali walked past her, up the few stairs and into the trailer. She found her vest, eased her arms into it, and zipped it up.

"Ali . . ." Her mother followed her back into the trailer. She sounded more tired than angry. "Your lungs can't take it; you know that."

"Mama . . ." She flipped the compression switch. The machine made a gentle whirring sound and the vest began to inflate. "I've gone two years riding this tour without so much as a friend." Her tone was soft; she had no desire to fight. "I think it's okay if I hang around one time to talk, don't you?"

Her mother hesitated. Then she kissed the top of Ali's head. "I want you well, Ali.

115

As long as possible."

"I know." Their eyes met. "I'm sorry."

Ali spent the next hour angry with herself. She shouldn't have asked Cody to come. She was wrong to invite him; wrong to make him think she was even a little interested. A friendship with him wouldn't lead anywhere, not when her health was so unstable. There was no reason to involve him.

The knock came at eleven on the dot.

Her mother was long since asleep. Ali pulled a jacket on over her sweater, opened the door and slipped outside, down the steps so that she was standing in front of him. "Hi."

"Hi." Cody took a step back, giving her space. He wore his heavy PRCA jacket, jeans, and a cowboy hat. It was easy to see why the girls never left him alone.

"My mom's asleep." Ali shut the trailer door.

"Oh." He stuck his hands in his pockets.

The night was the warmest it had been all season, and a slight breeze played in the distant trees. The parking lot floodlights were off. The only glow came from a canopy of stars and a sliver of the moon hanging on the horizon.

"Follow me." She led him around the

front of the trailer where two canvas chairs were set up. It was the place where she and her mother would sometimes sit and talk while they waited for Ali's events.

She took one of the chairs and he took the other, sliding it so it would be closer to her. "I got eight." His voice was a whisper.

"I know." She angled herself so she could see him better.

"You left."

"I came back." Ali studied him. Was he interested or only curious? Either way she had no business leading him on. "You were good."

A smile danced in his eyes, one she could see even in the dark. "Just following advice, ma'am." He shrugged one shoulder. "Sure glad you said something."

She grinned. "I do what I can to help." Her lungs wanted a full breath, but she could only take in so much air. She should've felt better after an hour with the vest. Her grin faded. It was a reminder she should keep the conversation brief. "Okay, you wanted to talk."

He hesitated. "You were gonna tell me why you ride sick." He leaned closer, his voice quiet. "Maybe you should get an inhaler or something."

She smiled. Four inhalers lay in a drawer

inside the trailer. "I ride because I love it, Cody. Same as all of us." Her hair blew in the breeze and she caught it, smoothing it back. A tinny Hank Williams song played from a nearby trailer, and the smell of horses hung in the air. "I just get sick more." She hesitated. How much should she tell him?

Cody stretched his legs, his boots almost touching hers. "Doesn't it make you worse, riding when you're sick?"

"If you were sick, you'd ride anyway." She stared at the moon for a minute, then back at him. "Right?"

He leaned back, locked his fingers together and placed them behind his head. "I guess." He narrowed his eyes, more concerned than curious. "Why are you sick so much?"

She blinked, waiting. "That's the question I never answer."

"I know." He angled his head, his eyes searching. "That's why I'm here."

"Hmmm." She pressed into the canvas chair. For the wildest moment, she actually considered it. What if she told him? Her secret had belonged to her and her parents all these years, but somehow — in the dark night with Cody Gunner — she wanted him to know. Maybe then he would lose interest; it would be easier than telling him later.

One thing was sure. Her secret would be safe with him. Cody talked to no one, same as her. If anyone could keep her situation under wraps, he could.

"Tell me, Ali." He leaned closer.

The smell of him was intoxicating. Leather and cologne, and something Ali couldn't make out. Confidence and charisma. The intangible that made every bull rider larger than life. The scenario played out in her mind. What would it hurt? She could have a friend on the tour, couldn't she? Someone who would know what she was up against?

Her hands trembled and her heart raced. She sat up straighter in the chair and met his eyes. "I have cystic fibrosis." There. She'd said it. She pulled her knees up and hugged them to her chest, her eyes still on his. "It's a lung disease."

Cody stared at her, his eyes wide. "Cystic fibrosis?" His expression changed from shock to anger and back to shock again. "Is it bad?"

Ali wasn't surprised at his question. Most people her age didn't know about CF unless they had a reason to know. "Yes." She rested her chin on her knees, but it did nothing to ward off the chill in her heart. "Cystic fibrosis is always bad."

His expression was frozen, as if he were waiting for her to laugh out loud and tell him it was all a bad joke. "You're serious?"

"Serious." She felt herself relax. Relief and a new sort of camaraderie flooded her soul. It felt wonderful to finally tell someone the truth. "That's why I cough so much; it's why I ride sick." She smiled. "I have no choice."

He was still motionless. His mouth was open, but it took a long while for the words to come. "Will you die?"

"Everyone dies." She kept her tone light. He didn't need to know everything.

"I mean it, Ali. How sick are you?" This time something vulnerable flashed in his eyes, a depth of emotion that couldn't have been easy for someone as private as Cody Gunner.

"I'm sorry." She sat straighter and gripped her knees, not sure what to say. Was she really having this conversation with him? Sitting beside him in the dark parking lot outside the arena, sharing secrets she'd kept all her life? She bit the inside of her cheek. "CF doesn't have a pattern. It'll shorten my life, yes. But no one knows exactly how much."

He stared at her for a few more heartbeats. Then he stood and walked a few feet away, his back to her. His outline was impressive in the shadows, the cowboy hat and jacket only adding to his image. He wasn't going to stay, she could tell. Her honesty had frightened him. They probably wouldn't talk again after this.

"Cody?"

He turned, hung his head for a moment, then straightened and returned to his chair. A long sigh left his lips as he looked at her again. "I'm sorry."

"Don't be." She lowered her voice. If they weren't careful her mother would wake up. "I'm doing what I love. How many people can say that?"

"Riding horses." He lifted his hat and pushed his fingers up his forehead and into his short hair. His voice was tinged with pain and frustration. "That can't be good for you."

The breeze was picking up, the temperature dropping. "Anything that makes me feel that alive is good for me." Ali eased her feet back to the ground. "I get sick once in a while, but the doctors know what to do for me."

"That's why you were gone a few weeks ago?" The reality of her situation was settling in. The shock was gone, and now his eyes held a helplessness, a futility.

"Yes. I spent a week in the hospital. Sort of a tune-up." Ali turned toward him in her chair so she could see him better. "I wear a compression vest three times a day. Otherwise my lungs will get worse."

"So that's . . ." He swallowed, his eyes wide. "That's why you go straight to your trailer."

"Mm-hmm." She felt utterly at peace. How wonderful to finally tell another competitor the truth, more wonderful than she could've imagined. Hiding her sickness had allowed her to compete like anyone else; but the journey hadn't been easy. Everyone wondered about her; they guessed about what made her different from the others.

Now Cody knew.

She explained how she held her breath when she rode, how she took only a few inhalations in the tunnel to keep from breathing in too much dust, and how she'd kept the entire ordeal a secret. "I never wanted anyone to leak it to the press. I wanted people to know me for the way I run barrels, not my sickness."

"Why me, Ali?" His eyes softened. "Why'd you trust me?"

"You asked." She looked at the silhouette of the nearby mountains against the sky. Then she found his eyes again. "You're a lot like me, Cody. All you need is the ride."

"Yes." Cody thought about that. "Can I do anything to help? Anything that would make it easier for you?"

She grinned. "Sure. Don't talk to me in the tunnel." She pointed toward a clearing a few yards away. "And could you ride your bulls out here so I could watch?"

His smile broke the tension of the moment. "If they'd let me, I'd do that every night. I hate the crowds. They're not why I ride."

Silence sat between them for a time.

"That brings us to you, Cody Gunner." She lived with CF every day of her life. She was finished talking about it for now. "What makes you so mad? I watched you tonight, all that anger. It has to come from somewhere." She waited. "What are you fighting out there?"

Cody studied her for a minute. "You should get in; you have goose bumps."

"I'm okay." She paused, wanting his answer.

"No. It's late." He reached out his hand to help her up. "I don't want you getting a cold."

The minute his fingers touched hers, she felt it. A current of something new and wild and exciting. Something that touched her heart and soul and body all at the same time. As soon as she was on her feet, she let go and the moment was over. Her cheeks were hot, and she was glad for the darkness.

"Okay." She swallowed. Was he really worried about the cold air, or had her honesty scared him? Either way, he was right. She needed to get inside. "Maybe some other time."

"What about tomorrow?"

"Tomorrow?" Her heart soared.

"If it's okay. I'll meet you here, same time?"

"Okay."

They stood, facing each other. For a long moment she searched beyond his eyes. She'd been wrong earlier. He wasn't afraid of her disease. They had found a friendship, and she was completely comfortable with that. He wouldn't tell anyone her secret. Besides, it didn't matter as much now. Dr. Cleary was right; her time on the tour was short.

Eventually everyone would know the truth about Ali Daniels.

"Thanks for talking." He slid his hands

into his pockets again. "Go in and get warm."

He hesitated, and she wondered if he was going to hug her. But then he took two steps back and tipped his hat. "Good night, Ali."

"Good night."

She was inside before she acknowledged the subtle ache in her chest. She was breathless, flushed, the way she felt when she needed her inhaler. Only this time the feeling was different, and Ali knew why. She wasn't breathless because of the night air or the long day or the battles she fought with cystic fibrosis.

She was breathless because of Cody Gunner.

Ali drove him in ways he didn't dare tell her.

That first night was the beginning of many. Through summer and into fall, for the rest of the season, Cody was driven by a different set of feelings. He enjoyed the bulls more, embracing the adrenaline rush and smiling more often when he lasted eight seconds. After a good ride, he would raise his fists to the crowd and grin at their applause, or toss his hat at a bull that had given him a winning ride. For the first time, Cody identified with the other cowboys on the tour. It was a rush, riding bulls, a rush Cody had missed too often in the years when every ride was consumed with thoughts of his father.

Now, when the familiar anger kicked in while he was lowering himself onto a bull, when it churned in his gut and made him grit his teeth during his final seconds in the chute, it was less about his father than something else, something new.

A lung disease called cystic fibrosis.

He and Ali talked about everything, and their talks became a lifeline, the difference Ali made in his life too big to measure. Because of her, he didn't go through the day angry, he didn't waste the nights putting out the embers of hatred with a six-pack. Rather he spent his days waiting for the one night each weekend when he and Ali could be together.

Always he'd known that if he fell for a girl, his riding days would be numbered. Because love was a light that wouldn't allow darkness to reign in his soul. And without the darkness, what reason did he have to battle it? To get in the arena with a snorting beast and fight for his life? Without the rage? There would be no point.

But with Ali it was different.

What he felt for her was more pure and honest, more intense. And it made everything about riding bulls more intense, too. It wasn't love, not in the conventional sense. His feelings for Ali were deeper, stronger, the same sort of emotions he felt for Carl Joseph. He would've protected Ali Daniels if it meant jumping in front of a train or taking a bullet in the chest.

Feelings that strong.

As the season played out, the two of them stayed near the top of the leaderboards. Since talk on the tour flowed like cheap wine, Cody kept his distance during the day. Neither of them wanted their names linked for any reason other than the obvious — they were both among the best in the business.

But at night, after the championship buckles had been handed out and the crowds had gone home, Ali and Cody would sneak out and take their places in the familiar chairs in front of her trailer. There they opened themselves to a world neither of them had ever known before.

The world of friendship.

He told her the story of his childhood, how his father had left, and how there would always be the struggle to forgive the man. Some of the more private details he kept to himself, sparing her the part about Carl Joseph's handicap and running after his father's cab and how he felt no connection with his mother.

Still, what he did share was more than he'd ever told anyone.

No matter how late they stayed up, whispering in the moonlight, they never ran out of things to talk about. Once in a while a comfortable silence would fall between them and Ali would smile at him, her eyes dancing.

"You aren't chasing me, right?"

He would raise his eyebrows in mock surprise. "Chase *you?*" His chin would lift a few inches. "Come on, Ali. I don't chase girls. You know that."

"Good." She'd pull her feet up, her voice full of teasing. "I don't want to be caught, remember?"

"Yes, Ali, I remember." He'd hold his hands up in surrender. "You're safe with me; I don't want to be caught either."

Ali Daniels was the most serious girl he'd ever known. But after a few weeks, he found ways to make her laugh. Before turning in for the night they'd sometimes be in tears from trying to stifle their bouts of laughter, keeping quiet so they wouldn't wake her mother.

By the end of the season they both quali-fied for the National Finals Rodeo in Las Vegas. Usually after a long year, Cody was anxious to get to the NFR, ready to take a shot at the title and head home. But this year he had no home to go back to. His fa-ther had moved in, and from what his mother said he was sleeping in Cody's bed-room. There was even talk that the two of them might get remarried. Apparently, Carl Joseph was thrilled.

Cody wanted nothing to do with any of them.

So instead of looking forward to the season finale, he was dreading it. Ali was coughing harder, looking tired more often. She wanted a national championship in the worst way, but her times had been a whole second or two slower in the past weeks. They would compete like crazy and when the final buzzer sounded he had no idea what he was going to do.

But that wasn't why he was dreading the final. He dreaded it because after the finals he wouldn't see Ali again until late January in Denver. The truth was something he recognized. He could barely last a week without her.

How was he going to survive two months?

Chapter Nine

For Ali Daniels, there was no worse place to compete than Las Vegas.

A constant wind blew across the desert floor, stirring up dirt and pushing the smog from one side of the valley to the other. The National Finals Rodeo was held at the Thomas and Mack Center, a huge indoor arena that sat more than fifteen thousand fans. Not only would the dirt be softer, more likely to fill the air, but NFR organizers used indoor fireworks before each day's events.

And the NFR didn't happen in a weekend like other rodeos throughout the year. It ran ten days straight. Ten days of racing barrels through dust and fireworks smoke and the stuffy confines of one of the biggest indoor arenas of the year. Even the locker rooms were worse, because officials at the University of Nevada at Las Vegas covered the tunnel and locker room floors with plastic. That meant the dirt wasn't packed down the way it was in most arenas.

No wonder she hadn't done well at her first two NFR showings.

This year, though, she had a plan. She would wear the compression vest ninety minutes, three times a day. The longer she spent in the vest, the more relief she felt, and the longer that relief lasted.

It was the first day.

She and her mother had found a nice spot at Sam's Town for their trailer, an oversized space with trees along one side. Ali liked that; it would give her and Cody privacy for their late-night talks. Cody had a room at the hotel next door, so after the rodeo each night, they wouldn't have trouble meeting up.

Ali slipped on her vest and zipped it up. She and her mother had spent the past two weeks at home, the first three days in the hospital. The doctor's warnings were just as strong as before, but he stopped short of badgering her. When the season was over, when she had her national championship in hand, then she could think about quitting.

Not until then.

She flipped on the compression switch and felt the vest fill up. At the same time, the door opened and her mother walked in, a bag of groceries in her arms.

"Again?" She set the bag down and began unloading it. "Didn't you get an hour earlier?"

"Ninety minutes. I'm going longer for the next ten days."

Her mother was quiet, unusually so. She finished putting away the food and took the chair opposite Ali. "Honey, we need to talk."

Ali felt her heart skip a beat. Her mother was easy. Whatever hardships being on the Pro Rodeo Tour caused, however difficult it was being away from home, her mother never let on. She wanted Ali to be happy. It was the reason she'd agreed to travel with her in the first place. But the concern written into her expression now was something Ali almost never saw.

"What's wrong, Mama?"

A tired breath made its way from her. "I was in line at the store, and two bull riders were in front of me."

Two bull riders? Ali wasn't sure what to say. She waited for her mother to continue.

"They were talking about Cody Gunner. One of them laughed about how tame he was these days, none of the partying and loose women he used to associate with."

Ali had a feeling about what was coming. But how could anyone have known? They hadn't so much as shared a conversation in front of the other riders. She swallowed. "Okay . . . I guess that's good, right?"

"There's more." Her shoulders dropped a notch. "The other cowboy said, 'You know what happened to Cody, right?' And the first guy nodded and said, 'Ali Daniels, that's what happened to him.' "

She blinked, searching her mind's list of possible replies.

"I'm with you all the time in the arena, Ali. Ever since that first night when you and Cody talked, I've watched you and seen nothing. Absolutely nothing between you." She turned her hands palms up. "Have I missed something? Are you dating that boy behind my back?"

Her secret meetings with Cody were never supposed to be anything but temporary, small chances for a friendship that had made the entire last half of the season her best days of all. From the first she'd looked for a way to tell her mother about her time with Cody.

Now she was getting her chance. She cleared her throat. "We're not dating, obviously. You'd know if I was."

"Then what? Why would they say that?"

"Because . . ." The vest made it harder to talk in whole sentences. She didn't want Cody to come between them. She closed her eyes tight and then opened them, her tone flat. "Because sometimes Cody comes by our trailer at night."

It took a minute for Ali's words to sink in. "What?" Her mother's voice was tight, disbelieving. "After I'm asleep?"

"Yes." Ali winced. Sometimes she had to remind herself. The vest wasn't squeezing the life out of her; it was pressing life back into her. "Yes, after you're asleep he comes by and we . . . we sit outside in the folding chairs."

Her mother's expression was a study in control. Shock and surprise added to the fine lines around her eyes. She wasn't angry. Hurt, maybe, but not angry. For a while the only sound between them was the steady rhythmic whirring of the vest as it worked on her lungs. What was she thinking? Was she disappointed, frustrated? Was she ready to take the two of them home for good?

Finally Ali couldn't handle another minute. "Mama? Say something."

Her mother leaned her elbows on the arms of the chair and looked at Ali. "Do you love him?"

The question made Ali hesitate, and that hesitation terrified her more than anything her mother could've said or done. Did she love him? Of course not, right? The idea was absurd, falling in love with a reckless bull rider like Cody Gunner.

But then why did she hesitate?

Ali ran her tongue over her lower lip. "No, Mama, it's not like that. He's my friend; nothing more."

Her mother's words were calm, deliberate. "Then why hide your visits? Did you think I wouldn't approve?"

"Do you?" Ali's answer was sharper than she intended. Her heart melted and she felt her expression soften. "I kept thinking about what you said. Heaven forbid it be someone like Cody Gunner. I didn't think you'd want me talking to him."

Her mother drew a slow breath, her eyes searching Ali's. "How much have you told him?"

If she was going to be honest, she couldn't stop now. "Everything. He knows about my CF."

"Well . . ." her mother slid back in her chair. She turned it so she was facing the opposite window. "It'll be all over the tour by January, if it's not already out there. If that's what you want, then I guess it's okay if —"

"Mama!" Ali was supposed to relax when the vest was on, work with the compressions so they were more effective. But she was too upset to relax. She flipped the switch and the machine fell silent. "Turn around and look at me. Please!"

Her mother spun around. "Don't use that tone with me, young lady. Cody Gunner's reputation precedes him. In the arena and out. He's not your type, not our type."

"Be quiet, Mama." Ali's voice rang with passion. "You don't know him. He won't tell a soul about my CF." She pressed her hand against her chest. "He'd do anything for me. Anything at all."

Her mother's mouth hung open. "Dear me." The words were the slightest whisper. "You're in love with him and you don't even know it."

"I'm not in love with him. He's my friend. The first friend I've had since I started riding professionally." Ali's throat was tight, her lungs heavier than usual. "Can't I have that, Mama? One single friend?"

For years, her mother had been forced to hold back her opinions, forced to let Ali make her own decisions about the way she spent her time. Even when those decisions might take years off her life. Now, Ali could see the same struggle playing out. Her mother didn't want Cody Gunner around any more than she wanted Ali on a horse.

She crossed the small space between them and knelt at Ali's feet. With gentle movements, while her eyes filled with tears, she put her hand on top of Ali's knee. "I'm sorry, honey. I never meant to upset you."

Ali put her arms around her mother's neck. "I don't love him, Mama. I promise." Tears filled her own eyes, because it wasn't fair. She was twenty years old and she wouldn't see thirty. Tears because her mother had given so much, and now she was afraid Ali would somehow share what was left of her time with Cody Gunner.

"It's your life, Ali." She whispered the words against Ali's cheek. "I promised you a long time ago — I won't tell you how to live it."

There it was. The bottom line, the thing her mother always said whenever they had these discussions. After Anna's death, when the idea of horseback riding seemed suicidal, time and again when Dr. Cleary insisted that barrel racing would cut years off her life, and now — when Ali wanted the green light for a friendship with Cody Gunner.

Ali closed her eyes and a stream of hot tears spilled onto her cheeks. Her mother's words ran through her mind again. *It's your life, Ali . . . I won't tell you how to live it.* Exactly what she needed to hear.

"It's okay, honey." Her mother took her hand and squeezed it three times. Their silent way of saying the three most important words of all, *I love you.* "It's okay."

She sniffed and blinked her eyes open. "Can I have him come earlier tonight? Before you go to bed."

"Yes." Her mother reached out and dried her cheeks. "I'd like that."

Ali took second that night, putting her in position to make a run for the championship. She had only a minute to pull Cody aside and tell him about the conversation with his mother.

"She must hate me for keeping you out late."

"No." Ali shook her head. "Give her a chance. She's on our side, Cody. Really. Come by early tonight; you'll see."

At 10:30 he knocked on their trailer door, and Ali let her mother answer it.

"Cody." Her mother hesitated, but her voice was warm. "Come in."

From the back of the table where she sat, Ali felt herself relax. Everything was going to be fine, once her mother got to know him.

"Yes, ma'am." Cody's voice rang with cowboy respect. "Thank you."

Ali's mother stepped back and gestured toward the small table where Ali was sitting. "How'd you ride tonight, Cody?"

"I took third, ma'am. The bull could've been better."

"We'll be pulling for a better draw tomorrow." She gave him a smile that eased the tension. "Iced tea?"

"Yes, ma'am, that'd be nice." Cody shot a nervous glance at Ali. "I appreciate you having me."

Ali's mother was at the small refrigerator, pouring three glasses of tea. "Well . . ." She looked at him over her shoulder. "It's about time you saw the inside of our trailer."

The silence was interrupted by Ali's giggles, and not long after, her mother and Cody joined in. After that, the ice was broken. Their evening visits continued to be early every night that week, and always, sometime around eleven, Ali's mother would turn in. Ali would get into her sweatshirt, and she and Cody would find their familiar places in the chairs outside.

Over the next few days, most of their talk

was about the competition. Cody held a strong second place, but Ali was frustrated with her times. She wasn't riding as fast as before, and she didn't know why. Her times had her sitting at fourth overall, but she would need a few first-place finishes in the remainder of the races if she were to have a chance at the championship.

"You're still holding your breath?" Cody was sitting beside her, closer than when they first started meeting together.

"Definitely." She frowned and stared straight ahead. "I do the ride in my mind a hundred times a day; I can't figure out how to catch that extra step."

"Hmmm." Cody stretched his legs out and folded his hands behind his head, the way she was familiar with now. A grin started in his eyes and made its way down to his mouth. "Someone once told me the secret was anticipation." He bumped her arm with his elbow. "Sound familiar?"

She chuckled, careful to be quiet. "Must've been someone smart."

"Yes." He tapped her head, letting his fingers run along her hair for a few seconds. "And did I mention focus. She thinks focus helps, too."

"Ah, yes. Focus." Ali did an exaggerated frown. Focus had been easier before, back when her mind didn't share time between racing and thinking about her conversations with Cody Gunner.

At most rodeos they talked for a few hours a weekend. At this one, they were together that long every night. By the sixth day, she met him outside the arena.

"You're right." She anchored her hands on her hips and squinted at him. The sky was bright blue, the December day as sunny as any in July.

"Right about what?" He smiled at her, studying her.

"About my focus; it isn't there." She shifted her weight, hoping he wouldn't take this wrong. He needed to understand. "Let's take a few nights off, turn in early. We can talk when it's over. Maybe that'll help me concentrate."

"I'm a distraction, huh?" He gave a light laugh, but disappointment colored his eyes. He kept his tone upbeat. "Sure, Ali. Whatever helps."

"You understand, right?" She felt funny trying to explain herself. Neither of them owed the other anything. "This championship means . . . well, it means everything to me. I've waited all my life for it."

The next four rides were the best either of them had all season. Still, the competition was tough. Ali was in third heading into the final round, Cody a few points shy of first. He was the defending champion, but for him it would come down to the draw.

Minutes before her race, Ali climbed onto Ace and ran her fingers over his coarse blond mane. She spoke to him, low and gentle near his ears, the way she always did before a ride. "Atta boy, Ace. It's all yours tonight. All yours."

A million thoughts fought for her attention. Anna sitting by the window looking out at the neighbor's farm. *I wanna race through the forever hay fields and play hide-and-seek out by the tallest pine trees, and jump on that palomino horse next door.* And her mother agreeing finally to let her have the baby foal. *It's your life, Ali. I won't stop you . . . won't stop you.* And Cody Gunner with those crazy blue eyes wanting to talk to her. *Just once, Ali. Tell me why you do it; why do you ride so sick?*

She cleared her mind.

People in her position talked often about sacrifice, all they'd given up to get where they were. For Ali, of course, the sacrifice was something more than a missed childhood or the cost of spending hours a day on the back of a horse. The sacrifice would come later — in the years of life she would lose for her decision to ride.

From the first time she watched a rider race around barrels she'd believed she was better, faster. That one day the championship would belong to her. And now here she was, minutes away from taking it, owning it. This would be the fastest ride of her life; she could feel it in her bones, in the center of her being.

It was her turn to take her mark.

Like always, Ace was spirited, desperate for the go-ahead, the chance to tear out of the tunnel around the course he loved. He nodded and pranced sideways. "This is it, Ace," she whispered. "Faster. Faster and stronger."

She sucked in a full breath and held it just as they tore down the tunnel and into the arena. The two of them flew around the first barrel, cleaner, faster than ever, and Ali knew it was happening. The thing she'd dreamed of since she was eleven years old was happening here and now, and no one could stop them.

Ace pushed himself, his hooves barely making contact with the soft dirt as he rounded the second barrel. *One more, just one more.* Ali pressed into him, willing him to move. They were almost around the third barrel when it happened. Ace's foot caught the barrel's edge.

"No!" Ali screamed, and as she did she sucked in a mouthful of dusty air. She lunged toward the barrel, desperate to keep it upright. But it was too late.

In the corner of her eye she watched the barrel crash onto its side, taking with it her only chance at the title. A spilled barrel was something Ali rarely dealt with; certainly never in a National Finals Rodeo. The mistake meant a five-second penalty, and a score that wouldn't be in the top six for the round.

She couldn't feel Ace beneath her as she raced into the tunnel. It was all a nightmare, right? She was dreaming, and any minute she'd wake up and it would be time to go to the arena. Her eyes closed before she came to a stop. *No . . . no, that didn't happen. It can't end this way.*

That's when she realized something else was wrong. She couldn't breathe, couldn't draw a breath. Never mind the race or the lost championship, suddenly she couldn't think about anything but drawing in oxygen, meeting her body's desperate need for air. She must have taken in too much dust when she took a breath out on the course, and now she couldn't stop coughing.

She dismounted and grabbed her water bottle. Her knees were weak, and it took all her energy to stay on her feet. Dark spots danced in her eyes and she held on to Ace, coughing with no relief, certain she was about to faint and not sure if it was because her heart was breaking or because she couldn't quench the burning in her lungs.

She sucked in a long swig of water and forced herself not to draw a breath. *Calm, Ali. Be calm.* The coughing wouldn't let up, and she sprayed the mouthful of water across the floor. This had happened one other time, and the doctor had told her above all not to panic.

But even Ace was nervous, whinnying and giving her anxious glances.

She was too far down the tunnel to get anyone's attention, but clearly she needed help. The coughing had kicked into an asthma attack. She needed her inhaler, the one she kept in her equipment bag for emergencies. Only this was the first time she'd ever needed it after a race, and she wasn't even sure where her bag was.

Nausea welled up in her and she grabbed at a shallow breath. More coughing, and now she was doubled over. She was about to drop to her knees when she heard his voice.

"Ali!"

Her face was burning up, red hot from the exertion. She met his eyes, and saw the inhaler in his hand. She couldn't speak, couldn't do anything but grab it and shove it up against her lips.

The first two puffs, she could hold the medication for no more than a second. But then, slowly, she felt her airways relax. The third puff lasted longer and by the time she took her fourth, the coughing subsided. Everything ached, even her bones. She was dizzy from the lack of oxygen, and just as she swayed Cody caught her arm and led her to a bench a few feet away.

He took the spot next to her, stroking her back, brushing his cool knuckles against her hot cheeks. "Ali, you scared me."

She was too tired to keep her head up, so she let it fall on his shoulder. For all their late-night talks, this was the closest their bodies had ever been. Ali couldn't get a rope around her thoughts. She'd lost the biggest race of her life, but somehow her heart soared with possibility.

"I . . . I lost."

"I know; it's all right. You can get it next year, Ali." He gulped and she caught a strange look in his eyes, something she hadn't seen there before. "Are you okay?"

Ali took in a slow breath. "I couldn't . . . couldn't stop coughing."

"I saw the whole thing." He smoothed a section of hair off her forehead. "The barrel went over and you breathed, didn't you?"

A sense of awe joined the emotions already having their way with her. She sat up straight and looked at him. "You saw that?"

"Yes." He exhaled, and she caught a look at his legs. He was trembling. "I knew you were in trouble; I ran for your bag, and your mom was already on it. She handed me your inhaler because I could get it to you faster." He ran his hand along her back again. "You sure you're okay?"

"I'm fine." Her heart rate was fast, but her breathing was as good as it would get inside the stadium. "Thanks."

He shot a look toward the arena. The floor was cleared already, the bull riders getting ready. When he spoke, his teeth were clenched. "I hate that you suffer like this, Ali. It isn't right."

Tears stung at her eyes, but she refused them. Rodeo riders didn't hold on to the hurt very long. It was part of their way, their lifestyle. She gave him a gentle push.

"Go ride. At least one of us can be champion."

Cody hesitated, looking into her eyes. "Later?"

"Yes." She didn't have to ask what he meant. They'd avoided each other the past four days, and in the end it hadn't done her any good. She didn't have a national championship, but she had a friend.

He gave her one last look, a grimace that shouted fierce determination. Then he stood, pressed his hat onto his head, and took off down the tunnel.

Her mother came through the locker room door at the same time, her face tight with worry. "I knew you were coughing. I gave Cody your inhaler; he could reach you first."

"Yes." She stood and faced her mother. The way her throat closed up, it was much worse than coughing, but there was no reason to say anything now. "Thanks."

They were talking around the obvious, but the pretense could only last so long. Her mother knew more than anyone how much the championship meant. Her health wasn't holding up the way she wanted it to, and unless she found a way to get stronger, she might not be well enough to compete next year.

Her mother's eyes grew watery and she held out her hands. "Come here, Ali."

Ali was tough so much of the time, determined to push ahead, bent on being the best barrel racer in the world. But right now, she didn't feel tough or determined or even close to the best in the world. She took a few steps and leaned into her mother's embrace, but even then she kept the sobs at bay.

She wanted to head back down the tunnel, find a spot with a good view and watch Cody ride. He'd drawn a tough bull, one that would give him the win if he lasted eight seconds. But at that moment, still buried beneath the weight of her defeat, in all the world she really needed just one thing.

To be held by her mama until everything felt right again.

Chapter Ten

Sling Shot was the best draw Cody had gotten all week. The animal was the biggest, meanest bull at the NFR, a bull with thick, curved horns and shoulders that could toss a cowboy across the arena in a single violent motion.

It was the exact draw Cody had been hoping for.

The rage he felt when he thought about Ali was almost frightening. She was an angel, a delicate flower with a grace and strength on horseback that would take the breath from anyone with eyes.

No one knew she was sick, because she didn't look sick. Her skin was tanned from the summer season, her pale blonde hair long and healthy. How would any of the others have known that the cough she battled wasn't a cold or an allergy, but a dreaded disease?

Ali Daniels shouldn't have had cystic fibrosis. She should've been dreaming of another five years on the tour, and then a life that was nothing but blue skies and flaming red sunsets. It wasn't fair, the disease. The ride beneath him was no longer tied in any way to his hatred for his father, but to cystic fibrosis, with all the merciless damage it was doing to Ali. Because it was that — combined with a reckless abandon for the rush of the ride — that had Cody riding better than ever in his life.

Cody positioned himself over the bull and stared at the animal's center. If only he could battle her disease the way he was about to battle the bull.

"Ready, Gunner?"

"Ready." Cody worked the muscles in his jaw and slid his mouthpiece in place. His blood boiled hot through his face and neck, down his arms. He lowered himself onto the animal's back, wrapped his hand tough and fast, and slid forward. Sling Shot reared his head back and lifted off his front feet.

Cody smacked the bull's neck, and the animal dropped, startled. "That's right." Cody seethed the words. No disease would ever hurt Ali Daniels, not if he had anything to say about it. This time he didn't wait. He shoved his crotch against his riding hand, leaned forward, and nodded hard.

The latch opened and the bull took to the air, spinning halfway around before ever touching ground. He was already twisting in the other direction as he pushed off his back feet. Cody kept his seat, his body so balanced he didn't feel like he was riding the bull, but floating above him.

A jerk of his neck and the bull was airborne again. Adrenaline surged through Cody's body and in that moment he believed he was actually stronger than the bull. Stronger and smarter.

Fight me, bull; try it. Ali would get on a horse again next season. Nothing would stop her, not even cystic fibrosis. Twice more the bull spun and bucked, arching through the air, and suddenly Cody knew. He had this one, the ride was his. He heard the buzzer. He'd made it; he'd ridden a bull that was responsible for some of the worst wrecks in the PRCA, and it had felt easy.

He leaned forward, readying himself. Next time the bull bucked he'd make the jump. The animal rocked back and then slammed down on his front hooves, his back legs snapping behind him. Cody pushed off, but as he did, the bull snapped his head back and caught Cody in the forehead with his horn.

A splash of dark spots filled his vision, but only for a few seconds. He felt one of the bullfighters at his side, helping him out of the arena. The other one must've been distracting the bull. Cody blinked and the stars faded. Blood was dripping down his face before he could get back to the gate. The doctor was at his side in three seconds with a cloth and a stitch kit.

He handed Cody the rag and helped him press it against his head. "Nice gash." He led Cody down the tunnel to the training room. "You okay?"

"Yeah." Cody wasn't sure what he felt. His head hurt, but it was nothing compared to the way his heart felt. Yes, he was the national champion bull rider, an award he'd won before, one he'd earned. But what about Ali? She'd wanted the title more than any other rider. How was that fair?

She was the best barrel racer on the tour, no matter what the final standings showed. He took a seat at the trainer's table. Like so much about her life, she deserved more than a seventh-place finish.

The doctor took the bloody cloth from Cody and studied his head. "It's deep, but not too long. Most of it's in your hairline." He chuckled. "We won't need to make a mess of that pretty face of yours. Not this time."

"I guess."

The doctor went to work, and Cody didn't flinch as the stitching got under way.

"You cowboy up better than anyone out there, Gunner." He wiped a clean cloth along Cody's brow, and dropped it on the floor. It was bloodred. "Blow like that should've knocked you out."

"I'm fine." He played the doctor's words in his mind again. *Cowboy up.* It was the slogan of the Pro Rodeo Tour, the slogan of bull riders and rodeo competitors at every level of the game. No matter how hard the hit, whatever the level of injury, a cowboy didn't stay down. He got up and shook off the pain.

Cody had ridden with broken ribs and a separated shoulder. He'd seen cowboys get knocked out, stitched up, and taped together and an hour later be rubbing resin into their rope, ready for the next go-round. Guys would laugh off the injuries, slap one another on the back, and say it again: "Cowboy up." The words had come to define the cowboy mentality, the rodeo way of life. Riders had two choices: cowboy up or go home. If cowboys didn't look past their injuries, the rodeo would no longer exist. Everyone rode hurt; it was the nature of the sport.

But the doctor was wrong. Cody wasn't the toughest cowboy on the tour, not by far. Not him or any of the bull riders or saddle bronc guys. He knew a competitor who could cowboy up better than any of them.

The rider was Ali Daniels.

Who else would consider competing week after week, knowing that every day on her horse took days off her life? Where was there another rider who raced without drawing a breath, who spent hours in a compression vest just so lungs would carry her through fifteen seconds of competition?

The doctor finished up and Cody headed back down the tunnel toward the arena. In a ceremony fitting of the NFR, Cody was named champion bull rider, and the crowd rose to their feet as he accepted his buckle. He grinned and held it up, waving first in one direction, then the other, giving them the reaction they expected. The reaction they deserved.

But all he could think about was Ali. How was she feeling? Was her breathing back to normal, really back to normal?

And what was she doing right then? He scanned the crowd, looking for her along the fence, but he didn't see her.

For the next hour he smiled for two dozen cameras, gave eight interviews, and signed autographs. The questions were the same every time. No, he wasn't hurt; yes, Sling Shot had been a good draw. Yes, of course he'd be back next year. No, he wasn't making the shift to the PBR, not yet. No, he didn't have any special secrets to staying on a bull — none he would talk about, anyway.

They were boring answers, and not altogether true. But they were the answers Cody always gave. The whole time Ali was on his mind and in his heart. He'd gladly trade in his buckle and prize money, his championship, if she could have another chance to ride, to prove no one was better. And since he couldn't do that, he'd do what was second best. He'd help her stay healthy; push her so she'd win it next year.

It was after 11:30 when Cody finally stepped out of the pickup truck of one of the steer wrestlers and headed for the Sam's Town RV lot. The air was warm that night, warmer than it had been all week. He wanted to take Ali out to dinner or go for a walk with her. But the casinos were terrible, thick with smoke and people. And it was too late to take a walk.

He heard high-pitched voices behind him. "Cody . . . Cody, wait!"

Girls. He glanced over his shoulder. Four of them were running toward him, three blondes and a brunette, and all looked to be in their late teens. One of them was waving something that looked like a hotel key. Disgust smacked him in the face. How many times had he taken advantage of a situation like this?

"Ladies." He waved once, tipped his hat, and kept walking. His pace was faster than theirs, and eventually they gave up. The last thing he needed was a group of fans following him to Ali's trailer. He pressed his hat low onto his head, careful not to tear the bandage off his forehead.

Be awake, Ali. Please. He squinted in the darkness and even from fifty yards away, he spotted her trailer and the single light she left on. The light that meant she was waiting for him. He jogged the rest of the way, and knocked just once on her trailer door.

She poked her head out and tiptoed down the steps. For a long time she looked at him. "Okay." Her eyes shone in the moonlight, the disappointment from earlier gone completely. "So I was wrong."

This was what he loved about her, that even when things could've been dark and somber, she found ways to play with him. The serious girl she'd been when they first started talking was gone forever.

He leaned against her trailer, breathless and grinning. "The nine-second thing?"

"Yeah." She winced and lifted his hat enough to see the bandage. "Maybe eight's enough after all."

"That'll teach me to listen to you." He adjusted the brim again. "Does that mean you were there?"

"Mama and I watched it from the press seats." She angled her head, her eyes full of admiration. "You deserved the win, Cody. You were brilliant tonight."

"Thanks." He gave a quick look over his shoulder, making sure the fans hadn't followed him. He'd been waiting all day for this time with Ali. He led her toward the chairs. "Let's move to the other side; it's quiet there."

They each grabbed a chair and set them up between her trailer and the trees. Her mother's room was on the opposite end, so there was no danger they'd wake her. Before they sat down, he turned to her and felt his smile fade. "I'm sorry about earlier.

You . . ." He looked down for a minute, the frustration back in full force. "You deserved it, Ali. What happened was wrong."

"I've thought about it." Her voice was clear and sweet, quiet against the night breeze. "It was my own fault. I tried to cut the last corner."

He looked up and met her eyes, and there in the moonlight he could see to the very center of her soul. "You have to come back, try again, okay?"

She swallowed, hesitant. "I will."

Something in the air between them changed. He was more aware of her than ever before. They were inches from each other, hidden in a place where no one could see them. "I wanted you to win, Ali." He looked down at her, his words a whisper. "You have no idea how much I wanted it for you."

She nodded. "Me, too." Her eyes held his, and this time he could see the sorrow, the depth of the loss and all it had meant to her.

Since he got there, he'd wanted to take her in his arms. And now he couldn't wait another moment. "Ali . . . don't give up." He put his hands on her shoulders and then pulled her in, folding his arms around her, holding her close.

In the past they'd been careful with the line between friendship and something more. In Cody's mind, the line was a wall, solid stone and ten feet high. A hug like this one would be over as soon as it started.

But neither of them was letting go.

Seconds passed, and the feel of her body against his shot a fire through him, a fire that was way beyond his control. This was territory they hadn't explored, and the dangers were there for both of them. Still, he couldn't let go of her, couldn't find the strength to pull away.

"All my life I've wanted that title." Her body trembled, her arms still tight around his waist. She pulled back enough to see his eyes. Her chest rose with every breath, and a mix of fear and desire filled her eyes. "But you know what?"

"What?" He could feel himself drawing her closer.

"I want this more."

"Ali . . ." What were they doing? They'd agreed things wouldn't go this way, not ever. But then why was he helpless to stop it? He ran his fingertips along her brow, her cheekbone. He inhaled, shallow and ragged. "This is when you're supposed to ask me."

Her eyes melted into his, and she brought her hands up alongside his face. "Ask you what?"

"Whether I'm chasing you." His knees were weak. He wanted to kiss her; he couldn't hold out much longer. His mind bounced between walking away, telling her good night and forgetting they'd ever come even this close — or giving in to his desire.

"Except" — her voice was breathy — "guess what?"

"What?" Cody swallowed, trying to believe she was really in his arms. He couldn't take his eyes from her. She was so beautiful, inside and out, more beautiful than anyone he'd ever known.

"It's okay." She lifted her face to his. Lilacs grew among the trees that lined their trailer space, and the late-night air was sweet with the smell of them. Then without waiting, she drew him closer and kissed him. It was a soft kiss colored with question marks, framed in uncertainty. The kiss of sweet inexperience and uncontrollable desire. "It's okay." She drew back, her eyes dark. "Because you already caught me."

Her kiss was still fresh on his lips, but this time he took the lead. Slow and deliberate, he shaded her with the brim of his hat and brought his lips to hers. He let the kiss build, guiding her, showing her the way until she was as involved in the moment as he was.

A minute passed before she started to squirm and then in a rush, she pulled back, her breathing fast and uneven. "Cody . . ." She stared at him, eyes wide, frightened. "I'm sorry. I can't . . ."

"It's all right, Ali." He moved closer.

"No." She spun around and took three steps toward the trees. "I didn't mean it." Her ponytail was loose; strands of blonde hair spilling onto her red sweater. She turned and faced him. "I didn't mean it, Cody. I don't want to be caught."

"Ali . . ."

"I don't." Her voice was louder than it should've been. She paced a few steps in each direction and then found his eyes again. "That . . ." She waved her hand in the air. "The way that felt . . . it scares me to death."

Cody hesitated. "Why?" This was the reason he hadn't crossed the line before tonight. He could handle being just her friend. But he couldn't stand her being afraid, upset.

Tears filled her eyes and she shook her head. "You don't understand."

"Yes, I do." He closed the distance between them. "You never wanted to need me, right?" His words were quiet, calm. "That's it, right, Ali?"

"No." She hung her head, the fight gone from her voice. "We'll both lose, Cody." She looked up. "If we let this happen, we both lose."

"You're wrong." He was closer now. "We both win." He wove his fingers into her hair and eased the band from her ponytail. Her hair fell loose around her shoulders, and with the slightest pressure from his fingers, he pulled her to him once more.

"Be my friend." She pressed her head to his chest, keeping a fraction of an inch between them, and at the same time clutching at his back, her heart and mind at odds.

"I will, Ali." He crooked his finger, placed it beneath her chin and lifted her face to his. "After tonight, okay?"

That was all he needed to say. Going against everything she was asking of him, she kissed him again. Long and with an intensity that hadn't been there before. When she came up for air, she searched his eyes and the understanding was clear.

They would have this night, this single time to pretend they could be more than friends, to believe that she wasn't sick and he wasn't determined to remain a loner. Cody leaned against the fence, the tree branches creating an alcove that belonged to them alone. Cicadas played softly in the distance, and a ribbon of cool air mixed in the breeze. He drew her close and for the sweetest hour they kissed and whispered and held each other, allowing the intensity between them to build until Cody couldn't take another minute.

"Ali . . ." He stepped around her and flopped into one of the canvas chairs a few feet away. He stared at the sky, his body burning with an intensity he'd never known before. A long exhale came from him and he chuckled, trying to cool off. Did she have any idea how she made him feel? "I have to go."

She looked at the ground, her expression shy and a little embarrassed. "I know . . . it's late."

His body screamed to return to her, but he had to get back. If he didn't stop now, if he didn't return to his hotel room, he would cross other lines. Lines he would never dream of crossing with Ali Daniels, at least not in sane moments. He rubbed the back of his neck and grinned at her. "That wasn't so bad, was it?"

"No." The shyness left and a grin tugged at the corners of her lips. "Not too bad." She brushed the back of her hand against her lips. Her eyes were still dark, her voice throaty. "We haven't talked about the Christmas break."

"No." Cody forced himself to stay in the chair. "I'm not going home this time."

"Where then?"

He shrugged. "One of the steer wrestlers has a cabin on his ranch. Maybe there."

"Hmmm." She came to him and took the other chair. "I have an idea."

Cody took her hand in his, running his thumb along the soft inside of her palm. He waited, watching her.

"My dad's looking for someone to help out on the ranch." Her voice was hesitant, but she continued. "He wants to be with me over the break." She met his eyes. "We have a guesthouse. What do you think?" She raised her brow. "Wanna spend Christmas with us, Cody?"

Two months on Ali's ranch? Days and hours of conversations and long walks and quiet laughter with her? Cody let the idea take root, and as it did the strange feeling came over him again, the one he couldn't quite pinpoint. He slid his boot alongside hers and tapped her toe. "Are you sure?"

"Mmm-hmm. I talked to Mama earlier today. She's fine with it; Daddy, too."

He leaned back in the chair, his eyes still on her. "What happened tonight, that won't happen again, right? That's the way you want it?"

Sorrow cast a shadow over her. "It's the way it has to be, Cody. I wish I could explain it better."

"I understand." He gave her a half smile. "At least I'll try to understand." Two months on Ali's ranch as nothing more than her friend? The situation would test his will. But the alternatives weren't even a consideration. He had no choice; he would take whatever she gave him. "When do we leave?"

A smile filled her face, the biggest smile he'd ever gotten from her. "First thing in the morning."

"I'll be here." He brought her hand to his lips and kissed it, the most tender kiss he could manage. His heart soared, breaking through the clouds of gloom and doubt and loss, all the feelings he would've had if this were good-bye. "See you tomorrow, Ali."

It was on the way back, halfway to the hotel, that Cody had a sudden realization. Since he'd known Ali, he hadn't been able to make out the strange feeling in his chest, the way she sometimes took his breath away and left him weak at the knees. Admiration, companionship, definitely. But this feeling wasn't that. It wasn't even lust.

Now, after an hour in Ali Daniels' arms, he knew exactly what the strange feeling was, and the realization made his head spin. He would have to keep the truth from her; otherwise she'd run scared away from him, as fast as she could in the opposite direction. The feeling was bound to scare her, because it scared him, too. She was sick, after all. Cystic fibrosis meant she wouldn't live as long as other people. But the fear wasn't enough to keep him away, not with this new understanding of his heart's feelings.

It was a feeling he'd promised himself he would never have, not for anyone other than Carl Joseph. But it was too late now. The way he felt for Ali ran deeper than what he felt for his brother, deeper than anything he'd ever experienced. His feelings for her were raw and alive and all-consuming.

Never mind his tough-guy image, or all the ways he'd been invincible on the back of a bull. There was nothing he could do to stop the way he felt. No matter what he told her in the coming months about being content with her friendship, he would be lying. The truth was, he didn't care about Ali Daniels only as a friend.

He was in love with her.

Chapter Eleven

From the beginning, Ali believed it was possible.

She could bring Cody Gunner home and enjoy his company, watch him work the cattle in the fields, talk with him at night and still keep her distance. She had to, really. Because first place in her life didn't belong to her or Ace or the Pro Rodeo Tour. It didn't belong to Cody.

First place belonged to cystic fibrosis.

The disease would determine the number of her days and the quality in the number. But it wouldn't determine the way she spent her life. Cody knew she wouldn't live as long as other people, but he had no idea how little time she had.

So it was up to her to keep things between them platonic.

It was their third day back, and they were in Dr. Cleary's office, Ali seated between her parents. Over the phone, he had recommended a hospital stay — four days at least. But Ali convinced him she was just as well off at home. She could stay inside where the air was clean, use a portable oxygen tank, and increase her medications. Besides, she'd be around Cody and her family. That had to be better than the hospital.

Now, they were talking about the possibility of a lung transplant.

"We have the test results back from earlier. Your father was a match." He checked his chart. "Your mother has the wrong blood type. The problem is, we need two donors if we do a live-donor transplant."

"Couldn't we do just one?" Fear lined her mother's face. She could barely speak. "Wouldn't that help a little?"

"No. The healthy lobe would quickly be infected by the diseased lung." He shook his head. "I'd want to remove her lungs completely. She'd need two donors." Another pause. "And I've checked your insurance. The transplant will cost tens of thousands of dollars out of pocket."

"We'll find the money." Her father gave a curt nod. The cost of cystic fibrosis was something he never talked about, something he seemed determined to protect her from. "Somehow we'll find it."

"Very well." The doctor went on about

the other details. Already he'd put her on a list, a registry through the University of Colorado Hospital in Denver where a computer would match donors with recipients. Most of the donors would come from cadavers, so there would be little warning if she was chosen.

The news was hard for all of them, but especially for her father. He was a quiet man, tall and strong. He'd missed out on much of Ali's barrel-racing career because they needed him back at the ranch, working the cattle. But during the times Ali was home, nothing would keep him from spending entire days with her — playing pinochle and backgammon and Scrabble while Ali told him stories from her year on the road.

But as Dr. Cleary delivered one blow after another, her father began to massage his throat. His cheeks got red; then his chin began to quiver. She'd never seen him cry, but when the doctor reached the part about the cost, and the last part — the part about still needing another donor to pull off a live transplant, two tears rolled down his leathered cheeks.

He cleared his throat and crossed his arms hard in front of him. "When . . . when will she need the operation?"

Dr. Cleary's lips formed a straight line. His eyes didn't waver as he looked at her father. "She needs it now, Mr. Daniels. Her lungs aren't getting any better."

"Maybe they will." Her mother put her hand on her father's knee. She tried to sound hopeful. "After she rests some."

Ali agreed with her mother. She was a week off one of the biggest rodeos of her life. If she could race barrels ten days straight, she couldn't be too sick.

"To be honest, I'm not hopeful." The doctor frowned. "Let's talk about the chances of getting a call from the donor registry." He crossed his arms, his jaw set. "Recipients are ranked according to their need. Ali needs a lung, but she'll live awhile without one. That means she won't be at the top of the list right away. The trouble is, once she's there, she won't have much time."

"What can we do, Doctor?" Ali's father took hold of her hand.

Dr. Cleary lowered his brow. "Live donors need the right blood type and they must be in good health. Healthy lungs have five lobes, two large lower lobes, and three smaller lobes. Ideally, donors should be bigger than the recipient, since their two lobes will replace five."

Her father had his hand near his throat again. "But if her mother isn't a match . . ."

"Then we need to find another donor." He looked from her father to her mother and back again. "Is there anyone in the family, an uncle or a cousin, someone who might consider being a live donor?"

Ali felt sick to her stomach, her head spinning. It was her fault they were having this discussion. She shook her head. "No. We can't ask that of anyone." She squeezed her father's hand and met his eyes. "We'll just hope for a call from the registry."

The doctor went through a few other pieces of advice and warnings, how important it was for her to stay inside and stay off her horse during the break, that sort of thing.

When the meeting was finished, Ali thanked the doctor. But she didn't say another word on the journey home. Her parents sat up front, with her in back. It was a seventy-mile trip to the hospital from the ranch, a trip she and her parents had made far too often. Ali kept her eyes on the road. She needed to be moved up the registry list; then everything would work out.

Her mother turned around. "What are you thinking?"

"Nothing."

For a little while, her mother was quiet, watching her. Then she reached back and put her hand alongside Ali's face. "God has a plan. He always has a plan."

Ali nodded and turned back to the window. She wasn't sure what to say. If there was a plan in her having CF, she didn't see it. After a while she looked at her mother. "I wonder if Anna's riding horses in heaven. You know, since her plan didn't include riding them here on earth." The sarcasm felt strange and bitter on her tongue, but her parents seemed to miss it.

"Well . . ." Her father adjusted his grip on the steering wheel and sighed, the type of tired old sigh that seemed to come from way down in his dusty boots. "I reckon she's riding the prettiest horse of all."

She glanced at her father in the rearview mirror. "How's the cattle work going, Daddy?"

He looked at her, his eyes dull, lifeless. "Cody, you mean?"

"Yes, sir. Is he working out?"

"He's a polite boy, hard worker." He stroked his chin, thoughtful in his appraisal. "I like him." His eyes caught hers and he managed a smile. "So long as you don't."

"He's my friend." She looked in the rearview mirror and grinned at her mother. "Right, Mama?"

Her mother looked slightly exasperated. She raised an eyebrow. "I have my doubts." She paused and her tone grew more serious. "You haven't told him, have you, Ali?"

"Told him what?" She wished her father would go faster; she wanted to get home and let Cody know the good news. No hospital stay for now.

Her father glanced back at her. "You haven't told him the truth about your health." He hesitated. "You're very sick, Ali. He doesn't know that."

"He knows." She kept her tone light. "I told him I have cystic fibrosis."

"But he doesn't know you could . . . you could be gone in a year, right?" Pain filled her mother's words. She didn't say them easily.

"Anyone could die in a year."

Ali's answer was quick, but her parents were right. Cody had no idea how sick she was, and she owed him the truth. They were quiet for a while, her parents letting the weight of their concern set in. As her father turned right onto their winding driveway, she let out a sharp breath. "Fine. I'll tell him."

"I just don't want him surprised." Her mother turned and met her eyes again. "You think the two of you are friends, but I've seen the way he looks at you. The boy's crazy about you, honey. Plumb crazy." She paused. "You need to tell him."

Ali agreed, but as she climbed out of the truck, as she spotted Cody on Ace a couple hundred yards away, she wanted only to run to him, climb up behind him and race like the wind across the fields, as far from the doctor's warnings as possible. She would tell him one of these days, before the next season started. Just not yet. Not with Christmas coming, not while they had eight weeks of good times ahead.

"Ali . . ." Her father stood near the passenger door. He seemed to notice the way she was watching Cody and Ace. "Go in now, ya hear? You need a treatment and a few hours of oxygen."

"I will, Daddy." She motioned toward the field. "I just wanna tell Cody we're back."

"That's not what Dr. Cleary —"

"Ali." Her mother cut in. "Do it fast. Please."

"I will." Their eyes met and what Ali saw made her heart swell. Her mother understood. It didn't matter if every outdoor breath cost her an entire day, nothing could keep her from Cody. The connection between them was that strong.

Her mother linked arms with her father and led him toward the house, her eyes on him. "A few minutes won't hurt; she'll be okay." Over her shoulder she looked back at Ali. "I'll get your vest ready."

"Thanks, Mama." Ali headed toward the field, but Cody wasn't where he'd been before. Maybe he'd seen them pull in and he was putting Ace in the barn. Ali kept her pace to a fast walk, dormant frostbitten grass crunching beneath her feet. Nothing that would make her breathe too hard. This was a period of recuperation, so any time outdoors was counterproductive.

She made her way to the barn and peered inside. He was there, leading Ace into one of the stalls. He turned when he heard her come in, and his face lit up. "You're back!"

"Yes." She wanted to go closer, but barns were the worst place for her. Even this one, with the air purifier.

Cody knew that. He left Ace and jogged across the hay-covered floor. "Let's get you out of here."

She nodded and followed him out the door and around the far side of the building, along the wall that faced the open land instead of the house. They stopped after a few yards and faced each other, leaning their shoulders against the wall. She stared at him, soaking him in.

"They didn't admit you." His voice was low, each word a caress against her soul. Barely a foot separated them.

"No." She grinned and raised her eyebrows. "I'm home for good!" She could barely remember the conversation at the doctor's office, not while she was looking at him, drawn to him. He smelled of cologne and hay and Ace's sweaty back.

He grinned. "That means you're doing good. Kicking CF in the shins, right?"

"I guess." She did a small shrug and suddenly, as it had the last time they were alone this way, the air between them changed. A stillness hung there, cold and crisp. Snow was in the forecast. Christmas was ten days away and everything about the moment was surreal, magical in a way Ali had never known before.

Cody felt it, too, she could tell by the way he looked at her. A force came between them, bigger than either of them, bigger than both of them combined. It drew them closer, paying no heed to common sense. Cody took his gloves off.

He stuffed them in the pocket of his coat and touched her face, her shoulder.

Before she could think about what she was doing, she was in his arms.

"Ali —" He looked into her eyes, searching her heart, her soul. His voice was husky, thick with emotion. "How can you ask me to be your friend? All I can think about is that night in Vegas."

She had no answers. She wasn't sure how she'd lasted this long. Every spare moment since that night near her trailer, even while she was telling herself she could keep her distance, she had longed for him, to be with him like this again.

Her eyes found his and her words were more of a cry than a whisper. "Kiss me. Please, Cody."

He leaned into her, his fingers warm against her face, and they came together in a kiss that was drawn out and fueled by desperate need. She nuzzled her face against his, refusing to pull away. He deserved to know what the doctor said, but she couldn't bring herself to tell him how little time she had. Not when all that mattered were the minutes they had right then, when she could still draw a good breath and he was so alive and strong and warm in her arms.

He kissed her again, brushing his lips along her neck, stirring up feelings wild and unfamiliar. "Ali . . ." He drew back and his eyes touched parts of her heart she didn't know existed. "I can't be your friend."

She let her forehead fall against his chin. "Yes, Cody. You can; you have to be."

"I can pretend, but don't you see?"

Her eyes lifted to his and her heart skittered into a strange pattern. The air was colder now, but it didn't touch the heat between them. "See what?"

His breath was sweet against her face, making her forget everything else. "I love you, Ali. We can take this as slow as you want." He kissed her forehead and both cheeks, looking like he was trying to memorize her with his fingers. "But nothing will change the fact that I love you."

Ali held on to him tighter. What had he just said? He loved her? Her feelings soared and dropped wildly in opposite directions, a part of her giddy, taken with his words. But an equal part terrified, because now, no matter what she said or did, there was no turning back, no way to pretend about a friendship when their hearts had moved miles beyond.

"I'm scared." She pressed in closer, sheltered by his presence, his feelings for her.

"Don't be." He found her lips again. His eyes met hers and she felt a strength, a power she could draw from, one she was no longer capable of. "Everything's going to be all right."

"Okay." She kissed him again. She wanted to tell him she felt the same way, that she loved him as he loved her. But the thought scared her to death. So instead, with every ounce of her resolve, she pulled away. "I have to go; my parents are waiting for me."

"Don't be afraid." He kissed two of his fingers and pressed them to her lips. "We can do this; we'll take it slow."

She nodded and moved another few steps back. Then she turned and walked quickly, steadily toward the house. Her cheeks had to be fiery red; certainly her parents would know what she'd been doing. But as she found the gravel path and headed for the back door, she wasn't worried about her parents.

She was worried about herself.

Because no matter what Cody said, he couldn't promise her everything would be okay. And what kind of person was she, letting him think they could be more than friends, letting him believe that love had a fighting chance between them? She was horrible, rotten, and selfish, but she could do nothing to stop herself. Her feelings for Cody were like a potent drug, and she the crazy overnight addict.

But that didn't make it right. Only Dr. Cleary could make promises at this stage in her life. And his words earlier that day meant just one promise remained for her and Cody. The promise that after today, only one thing could ever come of their time together.

Complete and utter heartache.

Chapter Twelve

For Cody, the days were torture.

Riding the fields of her family's ranch, tending her father's cattle, and all the while wanting to be inside with Ali. Once or twice a day Cody would go inside for a drink or a chicken sandwich, and always the sight of her took him by surprise.

She was set up in the living room, small plastic oxygen tubes running from a canister near her feet up along the side of her chair and into her nose. Most of the time she wore the vest, but once he walked in while her mother was beating on her back.

He stopped, horrified.

Mrs. Daniels had her hand cupped and in a methodical fashion, she pounded on a section of Ali's ribs. The blows came in small tight circles and when she had fully pounded on one area, Ali's mother would drop down a few inches and start making circles again.

After a minute, Ali saw him there and

gave him a weak smile. Her mother stopped and met his eyes. "Cody." She nodded, out of breath from the effort. "The vest can't get everything up. Sometimes we still have to do this."

Cody managed a brief nod and a quick glance at Ali, then he went to the kitchen for water. He gripped the kitchen counter and hung his head over the sink. Was this what she had to go through? Were the secretions Ali talked about that hard to remove? He couldn't imagine hitting Ali that hard, and yet . . . obviously the treatment worked. If someone didn't help her, her lungs would pay the price.

The scene made working with the cattle that much harder. He wanted to be inside, sitting next to her, reading with her or watching movies. She looked well enough, and the doctor's report had been good. But seeing her with the tubes in her nose, watching her mother pound on her back, Cody felt a thread of terror weave itself around the edge of his heart. She was okay, right? Better than before, wasn't that what the doctor had told her?

Nights were the best.

After her last treatment, she'd come off the oxygen for an hour or more. They would sit on the sofa, side by side, until her parents went to bed. Then they'd share quiet kisses and whispered thoughts.

Christmas came and they exchanged gifts. Cody gave her a white gold bracelet with a tiny row of diamonds, and she gave him a red scarf. Something she'd been knitting while he was at work outside. Two more weeks went by and Cody couldn't think of anything but her, his love for her.

She seemed to be getting stronger every day, her lungs more able to handle another round of rodeos. They talked about the upcoming season and how this would be her best chance to finally win the championship. But he couldn't imagine another year of hiding his feelings, sneaking out to see her for an hour or two.

It hit him one day, a realization as clear as the Colorado sky. He didn't want to be her secret friend; he wanted to be her husband.

The next morning he borrowed the Ford and headed into town. There, he picked out a brilliant white gold solitaire and had the inside engraved with one word: *Forever.* That night he wanted to talk to both her parents, but her father turned in early and Cody couldn't wait. Ali was upstairs taking a bath, so now was the time. With the ring in his jeans pocket, he found her mother in the kitchen stirring something in a green glass bowl.

"Mrs. Daniels . . ." He stood in the doorway, his heart racing.

She turned and looked at him. "Hello, Cody." A dishtowel hung over her left shoulder; her hair was pinned up.

"Ma'am, can I talk to you?" Cody walked the rest of the distance into the kitchen and anchored himself a few feet from her.

"Sure." She set the big plastic spoon on the countertop, blew at a wisp of hair, and turned to face him. "What's on your mind?"

"Well." His hands were sweaty. He wiped them on his Wranglers and reached into his pocket. The ring was there and he pulled it out, keeping his fingers tight around it. "Has Ali told you anything about the two of us?"

"Yes." Sarah Daniels' expression closed off some. "She tells me the two of you are friends." She raised one eyebrow a bit. "Nothing more."

He gave a nervous chuckle and ran his thumb along the ring, keeping it hidden in the palm of his hand. "To be honest with you, ma'am, things have changed. They've been changing for a while now."

"Changing?" She leaned against the counter.

"Yes, ma'am. See . . ." This was the hardest thing he'd ever said. Ali had been sheltered all her life because of her health. What would her mother think of her sick daughter falling in love with a bull rider? Cody clenched his teeth and continued. "I love her. I'm in love with her. We have . . . we have very strong feelings for each other."

Mrs. Daniels crossed her arms, her knuckles white. "Does Ali know you're talking to me?"

"No." Cody's answer was quick. "I went into town today and I bought this." He held out his hand and opened it. The ring caught the light and sprayed it across the kitchen. It was even more beautiful outside the velvet box. "I want to marry her, Mrs. Daniels. I wanted to talk to you and her father first, but since he was asleep I thought I'd show you the ring and —"

"No, Cody." She held her hand up and made short desperate shakes with her head. She brought her fingers to her face and covered her eyes.

Her obvious distress stopped him from saying anything else. He held the ring between his thumb and forefinger, and let his hand fall to his side. Was she that surprised, that upset about the idea? Was he such a poor choice for a husband that she couldn't hear him out?

Through the cracks between her fingers he could see the color leaving her cheeks. Her forehead was creased in a strong mix of grief and sorrow Cody hadn't expected. He felt his heart sink. Whatever the future held for Ali and him, it wouldn't be easy.

Finally, she folded her arms and drew in a shaky breath. When her eyes met his, he saw there were tears on her cheeks. "We asked Ali to tell you."

Cody felt light-headed. What was she talking about? Ali didn't need to tell anyone anything; that was his job. He was the one who wanted to ask the question. He blinked twice. "Tell me what?"

Ali's mother came closer and put her hands on Cody's shoulders. "Ali's dying."

He took a step back, letting her hands fall from him. Why would she say that, especially now? Ali was fine. She was better than she'd been at the end of the season. He shook his head, his eyes holding tight to hers. "That's a terrible thing to say, ma'am. Her doctor told her she was doing better."

"Cody." The woman's voice was tired,

but steadier than before. Fresh tears filled her eyes. "For years I've prayed Ali would fall in love, that someone might come along to make her forget about horses and barrel racing. Someone who would keep her indoors, where she could be safe." She made a sound that was more cry than laugh. "Instead, she met you. Someone who loves rodeo as much as she does."

"Ma'am" — he was shaking from head to toe, his world spinning out of control — "Ali told me about her disease. She said it would take years off her life, but she could live a long time still. Decades, even, right?"

"No." The sadness in her eyes was deeper, stronger than before. "Ali doesn't need a wedding, Cody. She needs a lung transplant. Otherwise . . ." Her voice caught and she brought the back of her hand to her mouth. Two sobs filled the space between them. She hung her head. "Cody, I'm sorry; Ali . . . Ali should've told you."

He couldn't draw a breath, couldn't feel himself standing there. It wasn't happening; he wasn't hearing this. He bent over, his forearms on his knees. *Breathe, Gunner. Get a grip.* Nothing was going to happen to Ali, nothing. He straightened and stared at Ali's mother. "What are you saying? She's sicker than she's let on?" His tone was angrier than he intended. "Is that it?"

Mrs. Daniels still had her hand near her mouth. She moved it now, her lips quivering. "Ali will be dead in a year without a lung transplant. *That's* what the doctor said the last time he saw us." She hugged herself and three more quiet sobs shook her shoulders. "We've all known it was coming."

Cody felt the wood floor beneath his feet buckle. Her words didn't make sense, didn't connect with the conversations he'd had with Ali even the day before. She was feeling better, anxious to get back on Ace, making plans for the coming season. Ali Daniels wasn't dying, not even close.

But that reality clashed hard with the one before his eyes. Her mother was crying, weeping for Ali and the pain she clearly believed lay ahead for all of them. He began to shake and sway a little. He couldn't get his words to come. Was it true? Could Ali have known this and kept it from him? Upstairs, the water was still running. Ali wouldn't be down for a while.

"Mrs. Daniels . . ." He waited until she opened her eyes, until he could see for himself whether Ali was as bad off as she'd said. "Ali won't live another year without a lung transplant? Is that right?"

"Yes, Cody." She looked at him, and in that moment he knew. "We've talked about a live transplant, but that won't work." A catch sounded in her voice. "She's on a donor list; that's all we can do."

Cody's head was spinning. It was true, all of it.

Ali's lungs really were that bad, no matter what she said or how she felt or how determined she was to be at the season opener in January. She was dying. And suddenly all the fuzzy lines of their relationship came into crisp, clear focus. Of course she hadn't wanted to be more than friends.

What had she told him that day, half a year ago, when he saw her riding Ace in the fields behind one of the arenas? She didn't want to be caught, right? But he'd gone after her anyway, even after she told him straight-up not to chase her. Only he couldn't stop himself.

And once he caught her, she couldn't stop herself, either.

A suffocating pressure settled on his chest, and he leaned his hip into the counter closest to him. There would be no wedding, no future together, not if she only had a year. Ali would never agree to it. She would cling to her thought that if she told him no, if she pulled away, she could somehow spare them both the pain that would eventually come.

The reality was still sinking in, still exploding through his heart and soul. Ali Daniels was dying. She was dying, and there was nothing he could do about it. Nothing he could —

What had her mother said?

Think, Gunner. There was a solution here; there had to be. She was on a donor list, but there was something else, right? Something about a live transplant, wasn't that it? *Live* had to mean someone living could give her a lung, at least it sounded that way. That would be serious, of course, but it could be done. And if it could be done then there was still hope; there had to be. He sucked in a full breath.

"Okay." He grabbed the thin string of hope and clung to it with his whole being. He studied her mother's face. "Let's get her a lung transplant. Then she'll be fine, right?"

Ali's mother closed her eyes and shook her head. New tears splashed onto the floor. "She's on a waiting list, but she's not a top priority, not yet."

His mind raced. He pinched the bridge of his nose, demanding his mind to focus. "Tell me about this live transplant thing. Why won't that work?"

She sniffed and brought her fist to her lips for a moment. "They can do a transplant with two living donors. Her father's a match, but I'm not." She shook her head and opened her eyes. "We've never been close to Ali's two aunts, and besides, she doesn't want to ask. She says it isn't anyone's fault but her own that she needs a transplant this soon." Defeat deepened the lines on her forehead. "Without a second donor the idea of a —"

"Wait!" The answer was easy. "I'll give her one of mine." Cody's heart pounded with hope. That was the answer. Of course it was. He could get by on one lung, couldn't he? People did it all the time. Hadn't he read about a rider who took a horn to the ribs, lost a lung, and kept riding? Or what about his grandfather? The man had lung cancer and lived another decade with just one lung. Possibility rushed through him. "I'll do it, Mrs. Daniels. I'll give her one. Then she can get better."

"Cody." Ali's mother came closer, her eyes begging him to understand. "Ali won't ever get better." She sucked in four quick breaths and gave another shake of her head. "A new lung will buy her three years at best. Three years, Cody."

Three years? Cody held his breath. It wasn't long enough, but it was better than one. And maybe sometime during those three years they'd find a cure, a way to help cystic fibrosis patients live longer.

Three years was an eternity if it meant keeping Ali alive.

"Mrs. Daniels" — his tone was calmer now, marked with a steely determination — "I've measured my whole life in seconds." He took her hands and squeezed them. His mind was made up. "On the back of a bull, eight seconds feels like a lifetime." A catch sounded in his voice. "Three years . . . ?" He studied her. "That's a thousand tomorrows, ma'am. Forever to a cowboy like me."

Ali's mother tried, but nothing she said after that came close to changing his mind. He turned in early, not sure he could face Ali without letting her know the truth — that her secret was out.

His conversation with her mother stayed with him as he headed for the guesthouse and long after the lights were out. He would give Ali a lung, and maybe she would get back five years or ten. Maybe someone really would find a cure. They could get married and force a lifetime of love and memories into whatever time she had. The more he thought about it, the more he was sure it would happen. And if it only bought them three years then so be it.

Because three years with Ali was better than all of eternity without her.

Chapter Thirteen

Before he could do anything else, before he could think about the future, he had to know if he was a match. The first test was simple. If his blood type matched hers, if he was healthy and bigger than her, he could be a donor. After that more specific testing would mix a sample of his blood with a sample of hers, to check for compatibility.

The next day he drove into Denver and headed for the office of Dr. Cleary, the man who knew how bad off Ali really was. A receptionist made him wait half an hour, but finally the doctor saw him. When Cody explained the situation, he was happy to draw the blood.

Cody had no anxiety while he waited. He knew the answer long before the nurse presented him with the results. He was a match; of course he was. He and Ali were so close their hearts beat in time with each other. How could his blood type have been anything but the same as hers? The other test results wouldn't be available for several days, but Cody felt confident.

That afternoon as he walked up to the house, he heard loud voices inside. He opened the door quieter than usual and listened.

"I don't care! You had no right to tell him."

"Ali, he loves you; he had to know." It was her mother. Cody sank against the doorframe and listened.

"I would've told him, can't you see that? How am I supposed to face him now?" She was crying, her breaths short. He wanted to go to her, but he steadied himself, waiting, listening.

"Ali, calm down. You do yourself no good by getting upset."

"I don't care!" She uttered a cry. "So where is he now, huh? Where'd he go?"

"I told you; he's getting a blood test." She sounded tired, deliberately calm, the sorrow from the previous night hidden, no doubt for Ali's sake. "Ali, he *wants* to give you a lung."

"No!" She shouted this time, her voice ringing with anger and fear. "I won't take it!" He heard footsteps and then the sound of the back door opening and slamming shut.

"Ali!" He heard her mother open the door again and shout after her. "It's too cold out there! Come back and talk to me!"

That was all Cody needed to hear. He ran into the house, grabbed Ali's black wool jacket from the chair, and exchanged a glance with her mother. "I'll bring her back."

"Please, Cody." Relief rang in her voice. "Get her inside."

Cody tore through the door in time to see Ali sprint across the backyard toward the barn. She was going for Ace, no doubt. Ali hadn't been on him since they'd been home, and he knew how badly she wanted to ride.

He had never seen Ali run on anything but a horse. Watching her now, he wasn't surprised. She ran fast, a picture of grace and beauty, the same way she was on Ace's back. He picked up his speed as she turned and dashed through the barn doors. By the time he made his way inside, she was already saddling Ace. She turned, startled by his presence.

"Cody!" She pulled the cinch strap tight, put her boot in the stirrup and swung herself into the saddle. Shame darkened her features. She led the horse a few steps toward him. A wheeze sounded between her words. "Go away . . . I want to be alone."

"I'm not leaving." He held tight to her coat. Then he closed the distance between them, grabbed the saddle horn and swung himself up behind her.

"Fine." She didn't skip a beat, but dug her heels into Ace's sides and leaned forward.

The horse took off like lightning, tearing out of the barn and out into the open fields. He could feel her shaking, shivering from the combination of cold and fury. His body sheltered hers, but it wasn't keeping her warm, not with the wind in her face. He leaned in and yelled loud enough for her to hear him. "Stop! You need your coat."

"No!" She shot the word at him over her shoulder, and leaned closer to Ace's neck. "Yah!"

The horse kicked into another gear. *Come on, Ali.* He gritted his teeth and hung on to the saddle with one hand. With the other, he draped the coat over Ali's shoulders, holding it in place so it wouldn't fly off. She kept Ace running, flying across the rolling hills and rocky bluffs toward the far end of their ranch. Only when she'd ridden past the cattle, out to the barbed wire, did she pull to a stop.

Without looking at him, she dismounted and walked to the nearest fence post. The coat was still hanging on her shoulders, and she bent over, coughing long and hard. Cody felt the fear rise in his throat. He didn't have her inhaler, didn't have any way to help her. They were too far out to get help if she couldn't catch her breath.

His heart pounded against his chest. "Ali!" He jumped down and headed for her. "Breathe out; it's okay. You can do this."

She was bent in half, coughing, gasping for breath. "Cody . . . I'm sorry . . . I didn't mean to . . . to hurt you."

"Don't, Ali. It's okay. I'm here; I'm not mad."

Her coughing was getting worse. The cold air and exertion must've kicked her into a spasm, because she couldn't catch her breath. She was heading into a full-blown asthma attack, the kind Cody had seen her suffer before. That meant she needed her inhaler, the one back at the house.

Her gasps were more strained now, frantic for air.

"Ali, breathe out. Come on, you can do this."

But she couldn't, and he had a decision

to make. He could get her back on Ace and go for help, but that would take ten minutes. Ten minutes they didn't have. If only she could relax, maybe the air would come.

His hand ran over her back, up and down in small circles. "Breathe, Ali. Please, breathe."

"I . . . I can't." Her coughing was horrendous now.

Terror filled him, paralyzing his ability to move or think or do anything but watch her fade away. He clenched his fists and shouted into the afternoon wind. "Help me!" His voice was lost among the rustling of pines overhead. "Make her breathe! Please!"

Ali coughed three times, but not as hard as before. She drew in a slow breath; it was raspy, but it was air. A tingling worked its way down Cody's spine from his neck to his lower back. He put his hand on her shoulder. His voice was quieter this time. "Ali, keep going! Keep breathing!"

"Cody . . ." She straightened some, her gasps farther apart. Now that he could see her face, the sight of her made him weak. Her skin was pasty gray, her lips a frightening shade of blue. "I'm okay."

He rubbed her back, leaning into her.

"Slow breaths, Ali. Slow and easy. Blow out; you're getting through it."

She rested against the fence post, shaky and weak. Her breathing wasn't normal but it was better. "Thank you."

He was stunned, speechless. If things had been different, she could be passed out on the frozen ground by now, minutes from death. He shuddered. "Here." He helped get her arms into the wool coat. "Let's get you home."

Their conversation came later that night, when she was rested and medicated, when all that was left from the terrifying afternoon was the memory of her anger.

They sat on the sofa, and Cody took the lead. "I heard you and your mother."

She crossed her arms and looked at her lap. "I wanted to tell you." Her eyes met his. "It was my job."

"It doesn't matter, Ali. I know the truth, and guess what?" He slid closer and took her hand in his. "I'm a match! As soon as you're ready, I'll give you one of my lungs. And maybe in the years after that they'll find a cure for CF and —"

"You can't." The anger was gone, but she shook her head anyway. "I won't let you." She bit her lip, her eyes damp. "You live for those eight seconds on a bull,

Cody. I won't let you give that up."

"I don't have to." He smiled, his tone confident. She couldn't change his mind any more than her mother could have. He was more convinced with every passing hour. "I called one of the rodeo docs and asked. He said a bull rider could compete with one lung." Cody didn't tell her the rest of what the doctor said. Riding with one lung was very risky; it meant less room for error. A punctured lung could be deadly in such a situation.

"But when, Cody?" She lowered her brow. "You can't take time off during the season."

"I won't have to." He ran his knuckles along her cheekbone. "You feel good, right?"

She studied him, puzzled. "So . . ."

"So we'll do the season together next year. When it's over, when we both have our buckles, we'll check into the hospital and I'll give you a lung." He kept a calm exterior, but inside he was holding his breath, pushing for her to tell him yes.

"Cody . . ." She angled herself toward him. "I don't want you to do it. You need your lungs."

"Come on, Ali." A grin tugged at his lips. He brushed a strand of hair back from her face. "We're talking about Gunner lungs here. One would be better than two on most riders."

She couldn't keep from smiling, even if fear still had the upper hand. "You're crazy."

"Yes. About you." He hesitated, watching her, waiting until the fear faded. "I'm doing this, Ali. I'm giving you a lung. I've already made up my mind."

"Cody . . ." The conviction was gone from her voice.

When she didn't go on, when she didn't argue or tell him she didn't want his offer, he knew he'd won. And with that, his heart shifted gears. He pulled the ring from his pocket. "Ali . . ." He leaned in and kissed her. "I don't care if you're sick, or how many years you'll get from a lung transplant." He kept his fingers on the sides of her face. "I love you."

The fear in her eyes turned to surprise, and the surprise to a sort of joy he hadn't seen in her since they came home from Las Vegas. "You really do?"

He slid her to the edge of the sofa and dropped to one knee. "I found out something today." He ran his tongue over his lower lip. "I found out I can't live without you." He kept the ring in his hand, tight against his knee. With the other hand, he covered her fingers. "But something else. Ever since my dad left, my mom has believed that someday I'd learn to let go . . . that I'd learn to love." He studied Ali, the picture she made. He would never forget the way she looked, sitting in front of him, healthy and whole. "And now look at me."

For the second time that night, a smile played on her lips. Her eyes held the now familiar adoration she hadn't allowed herself to feel since her angry ride the day before. She messed her fingers through his hair. "What am I going to do with you?"

He reached into his closed palm and lifted the ring for her to see. "Marry me, Ali."

Her mouth hung open for a moment, but her surprise gave way to a certainty that told him all was right with their world. She wasn't going to run or push him away. It was too late to keep from falling for each other. They'd fallen, and from this day on there would be nothing else.

Here, now, they wouldn't borrow sadness from some far-off day. Not when they'd found something so rare together. She slid closer to him and put her arms around his neck. "Cody Gunner, I have a question."

He brought his lips to hers, the gentlest kiss. Then he found her eyes, his voice barely a whisper. "Ask it."

"Okay." She watched him, her eyes full of light and love. Her smile started there and made its way to her mouth. "Are you chasing me?"

"Always." He grinned.

Her smile faded. "Don't ever stop." She kissed him with a slow certainty, a kiss that told him she had as much hope as he had about their future. When she pulled back, her eyes held a strange mix of starry-eyed dreams and smoldering desire. "Now I need to answer your question."

"Yes." He pressed his face against hers, holding on to the feel of her soft skin against his. "I'm waiting."

She giggled and leaned back, looking beyond his eyes and straight to the places of his heart that were no longer closed off. "Yes, Cody." Her eyes shone like never before. "I'll marry you."

He drew her closer, holding her tight not only in his arms, but in his soul. "I love you, Ali."

Her face grew serious. "I love you, too." It was the first time she'd said it. But once the words were out, the truth about them filled her expression. "I love you with all I am, Cody Gunner."

It was a moment that might've been marked by tears. But as they kissed, as she held up her hand and let him slide the ring past her knuckle, they laughed and held each other and whispered about what her parents would say, and whether he would even tell his. They cuddled on the couch, talking about wedding dresses and handwritten vows and honeymoons and the future, their eyes clear and dry.

Cody thought he understood why.

The story they were starting was bound to have sad scenes. The ending would be saddest of all. So why not smile and laugh and love as long as they had today? Why not admire her ring and kiss her and hold her, breathing in the feel of her against his chest? Today was no time for crying. Cody wasn't willing to lose a single happy moment with Ali Daniels. Soon enough down the road, the tears would come. For now, today belonged to them.

Today, and another year of rodeo, and after that a thousand precious tomorrows.

Chapter Fourteen

The Pro Rodeo season started out like the one Ali Daniels had always dreamed about. But even then she had a sense the good times wouldn't last.

She set a record at the opener in Denver, and took first place at all but two of the first seven stops. But along the way she could feel herself shutting down. Every breath required deliberate thought. Not just the breathing she did in the arena, but all the time, even after a long session in her compression vest.

They carried oxygen in her trailer, and Cody rarely left her side. He was first in the standings, riding with as much fury as ever — all of it somehow directed toward cystic fibrosis. At least that's what he told her.

At night he no longer stopped by for an hour. He slept on the sofa with Ali ten feet away in her room. She was surprised at the boundaries he kept for them. When their kissing stirred new and unspeakable passions in her, he would quietly pull away and bid her good night, even if it left them both trembling.

"I've done this my way before," he told her once. "You're different, Ali. I'd wait forever for you."

They set a date for their wedding — the third Saturday in May. There were no rodeos that weekend, and so they'd have most of the season to focus on gaining the lead in their respective rankings. The wedding would be small. A simple ceremony outdoors, atop a grassy bluff on her parents' ranch. Her mom and dad would attend, of course, but she wanted his parents to be there, too.

"Cody, you need to tell them." She'd bring it up every few days, but he shut down whenever she asked about it.

It wasn't until a California rodeo in mid-April that Ali saw for herself how angry he was with his parents. The arena was outdoors that week, and Ali was in the stands talking to her mother, the sunshine beating down on them, when a woman walked up and introduced herself.

"Ali Daniels?" The woman fidgeted, casting an anxious look over her shoulder. Behind her stood a young man with Down syndrome.

Ali smiled. "Yes?" She was approached by fans at every rodeo; especially now that she and Cody were an item. Half the time people wanted her to give him a message or have him sign something. But the woman didn't have the look of a fan, and something in her blue eyes was familiar.

"Ali, I'm Mary Gunner, Cody's mother." She held out her hand and gave Ali a nervous look. "I'm not sure my son would want me talking to you."

The boy behind her, the one with Down syndrome, was that Cody's brother, Carl Joseph? The one he had talked about? Her head spun and she struggled to find her voice. Why hadn't Cody ever said anything about his brother's disability? Ali felt an immediate warmth for Mary Gunner.

"Please" — Ali slid over — "sit down." She took her own mother's hand. "Mama, this is Mary Gunner, Cody's mother."

"Nice to meet you." Mary gave them a partial smile. She turned and motioned for the young man with her to take a seat. "This is Carl Joseph, Cody's brother."

"I've heard about him." Ali looked around Mary to the young man and waved. He had Cody's dark hair, but that was all. Carl Joseph's eyes were brown and deep set. He was thicker, stouter than Cody. "Hi, I'm Ali."

Carl Joseph raised his hand quickly and dropped it again. He struggled with eye contact, shy and grinning. "Hi, Ali. You're pretty."

"Thanks."

Mary patted her younger son's knee. Then she looked at Ali. "I got a call from someone in rodeo." She hesitated. "You and my son are engaged, is that right?"

"Yes, ma'am." Ali's heart went out to the woman. She wanted to hug her and apologize for the way Cody had shut her out. "We're getting married in May. I keep pushing Cody to call and invite you."

Mary folded her hands and let out a tired breath. "It isn't me he's mad at; it's his father." She hesitated. "We're back together now; we remarried over the Christmas break. But Cody can't think of his daddy without thinking about how he walked away. He won't return my calls, won't talk to either of us." Her eyes grew damp. "Mike Gunner's a different man now."

"Is he?" Ali had wondered about Cody's father. Whatever the man had done, Cody rarely got specific with the details.

"Oh, yes." Mary's smile reached all the way to her eyes. "He's wonderful, Ali. If

211

Cody only knew . . ."

"Mary . . ." Ali's mother leaned forward so the two could see each other. "Ali has cystic fibrosis. I wasn't sure if you knew that or not."

Cody's mother froze, her mouth open. The news took a few seconds to sink in, but as it did, her shoulders slumped some. Clearly she understood the ramifications of cystic fibrosis better than Cody had. Mary shifted her eyes to Ali, and placed her hand on Ali's knee. "I'm sorry; I had no idea."

"We've kept it a secret, but not for much longer." Ali's mother was stronger now, more accepting of the situation. "Ali has to have a lung transplant. We're planning the operation for December."

The pain in Mary's eyes was genuine, and Ali felt for her. After all the hurt the Gunners had experienced as a family, now this. Her son was marrying someone with a terminal illness. Next to her, Carl Joseph was blissfully unaware of the conversation. He cheered on the team ropers, caught up in the excitement of the arena.

Ali's mother wasn't finished. "There's more, Mary."

"More?" Heartache rang in her quiet voice.

"She needs a lung from two people, and I'm not a match. So . . . one will come from her father. The other . . . Cody wants to give her one of his."

Mary drew back a few inches, shocked. "Cody?"

"We tried to talk him out of it, but his mind's made up. He's been cleared by the doctor; he's giving one of his lungs to Ali."

A soft gasp came from the woman, and she looked from Ali to her mother. "Then . . . then that's the answer."

"The answer?" Ali's mother had tenderness in her voice. The situation was hard for all of them.

"For years I've wanted to believe that . . . that one day Cody would learn to love and now . . ." Her words caught in her throat. "I'm sorry. This is amazing."

Something caught Ali's attention and she looked up. Cody was coming toward them, staring at his mother, his eyes blazing. Ali stood. Maybe if she headed him off before he reached her, maybe then they could avoid a scene. "Cody . . ."

He stopped and waited, breathing hard, his eyes on the place where their mothers were talking. Carl Joseph remained focused on the arena. At that instant, the women both noticed him, and Mary started to stand. But before she could, Ali put a hand on her shoulder.

"I'll talk to him." The announcer was saying something about hot dogs being half price and Ali could barely hear herself. She raised her voice as she met Mary's eyes. "Thank you for introducing yourself. I . . . I hope one day we can work all this out."

She gave her mother a glance that said she'd be back. Then she went to Cody. He had his hands on his hips, his faded white cowboy hat dipped low. When she reached him, she took his hand. "Can we talk?"

"What's she doing here?" he hissed, his voice low.

"Follow me." She headed up the stairs and then down onto the dusty track that surrounded the arena. People were watching them, so she moved fast, leading him past the busy concession stands through the competitors' gate, to a quiet sun-splashed corner where they could be alone.

The whole time she could feel Cody fuming beside her.

She faced him now, her heart pounding. "What is it, Cody? Why do you hate her?"

His eyes narrowed. "You don't know everything, okay?" He seethed with each word, his anger reaching a level she'd never seen in him before.

But it wasn't enough to stop her.

She'd never pushed when it came to his parents, never dug deep enough to find out why his feelings ran so cold against them. She felt her own frustration building. "I might not know everything, Cody, but your mother loves you." She pushed her finger at his chest. "She loves you, Cody!" Her voice was louder than she intended, but she was too worked up to stop. "I saw that the minute she came up and said hello."

"Is that right?" He stood and glared at her. "Well, let me tell you something you didn't see." He was still furious, but he wasn't shouting. Other riders were looking their way. "You didn't see your father throw his suitcase into a taxicab and drive off without looking back. You didn't scream for him to stop, and run down the street after him. And you didn't stand on the corner watching that yellow cab disappear and never come back."

His chest was heaving, and anger wasn't the only thing in his tone. He had the eyes of a young boy, hurt to the core by the things he was sharing. Ali reached out and tried to take his hand. "Cody . . ."

"No!" He jerked away. "I'm not finished!" He turned away from her, took two steps, and faced her again. His cheeks blazed from the intensity of his emotions. "You know about Carl Joseph now, right?"

"You should've told me he was —"

"No." He dropped the brim of his hat another inch. "I didn't tell you because to me he doesn't have Down syndrome. He never had it. He's just a big kid with a big heart, but you know what my father said about him?" His words were fast, a string of bullets. "He said he couldn't be a father to a kid like Carl Joseph." Cody's eyes were damp, but he clenched his jaw, too angry to cry. "You wanna know why I'm mad? Why I can't run back home and pretend everything's okay? My dad left us because he couldn't love the most loving kid in the world, Ali. That's why."

Tears poked pins in her eyes, too. Her chest was tight, her airways too narrow, the way they got when she was upset. But she didn't want to move, didn't want to interrupt the moment by grabbing the inhaler from her boot. She didn't want to do anything but let him finish.

"Ali, you have no idea." He moaned and looked straight up at the sky, then just as fast his eyes found hers again. "You know what I never understood? The thing that drove me onto the back of all those bulls week after week after lousy week? I could see why someone shallow might not love Carl Joseph. Carl wasn't the perfect boy child, he wasn't the sort of kid a former NFL star could be proud of." He pounded his chest with his open palm. "But what about me, Ali? What was wrong that he couldn't love me?"

Cody dropped down slow onto his heels, and stared at the ground.

"There was nothing wrong with you." Ali coughed three times and then willed herself to wait. He deserved her full attention. She took hold of his shoulder; this time he didn't pull away. Three more coughs shook her chest. "It was your father, Cody. Something was wrong with *him*." She hesitated. "But maybe he's better now; maybe he's changed."

Cody jerked his shoulder from her reach. He lifted his head and glared at her. "Never mind." Disgust rattled his tone. His eyes were ice cold, the hurt from a moment earlier replaced by walls thick and immovable. He stood, gave her one last look, and turned around. Without saying another word he headed hard toward the stock area, his boot heels kicking up a small dust cloud with every step.

"Cody, wait . . ." A series of coughs

seized her, but she was on her feet anyway. She ran a few steps. "Cody . . ."

He stopped sharp and turned around. "Don't follow me." He spat the words, unconcerned with the way people stared and took paths around them. "You don't understand." He tossed his hands in the air. "No one'll ever understand."

"Hey . . ." She took another step closer, close enough to see the way his hands trembled. Panic took the tightness in her throat to a new level. She didn't have long. An asthma attack was coming. But right now the pain in her lungs was nothing to the ache in her heart. "That's not fair."

"But it's true." He spat the last few words at her. Then he turned and continued making his way toward the pens.

She coughed twice and watched him leave. There was no point following him, not if he wouldn't listen to her. She reached into her boot for her inhaler. What was he thinking? She was the only one who knew what drove him to ride. She'd spotted his anger before they had a single conversation. Of course she understood him.

One breath at a time she sucked in the medication, and eventually she felt her airways respond. She needed another session with her compression vest, but she was running out of time. The first round in the barrel racing was less than an hour off, and Ace wasn't warm yet. She turned and walked in the opposite direction, out to where Ace was tied up in a pen.

She tightened his saddle and checked his bridle. Then for the next half hour she loped with him across a field at the back of the parking lot. Ace was such a good horse, dependable and strong. Always there for her.

But what about Cody? Why couldn't he see that she was on his side? If he didn't make peace with his parents, the rift would always come between them. Family was family. It was wrong to go through life hating the people you were supposed to love most.

The air was humid that day, humid and thick. The pollen must've been high, as well, because Ali could almost feel herself breathing more than air. Usually the medication brought at least some relief. But this time her lungs were tight, stiff and unresponsive. The trouble was, she couldn't use the inhaler again, not for four hours.

"Okay, Ace, that's all," she cooed near his ears, resting her head on his. "Let's slow it down."

She walked with him a few minutes longer and then headed for the arena. Her race was sixth that afternoon; it was time to report to the judges. This rodeo was a big one for her and Cody. They both needed wins to head into the summer season in the lead.

Her chest hurt, and she drew a breath that didn't come close to filling her lungs. Warnings sounded in her mind. What if the race pushed her past the point of bouncing back? How would she get her mama's attention if she needed help? Ali checked her watch. Maybe she had enough time. She could go back to the trailer, use one of the vapor mist medications, maybe that would help.

Across the field she heard the announcer.

"Now's your time to get some popcorn, ladies and gentlemen, because we've got a treat up for you next. Some of the finest barrel racers in the business, including —"

Ali had heard enough, and in that moment she made up her mind. There wasn't time to go back. Her airways weren't in great shape, but she could get through the ride. Hold her breath and tear around the cloverleaf pattern. Then go back to her trailer and use the compression vest. Everything would be fine. In fact, as she rode Ace to the check-in point, as she readied herself for the race, she wasn't worried about herself at all.

She was worried about Cody.

Chapter Fifteen

He was an idiot.

No matter how angry he was at his parents, he had no right to take it out on her. What he'd said was right; Ali didn't understand. But that wasn't her fault. She hadn't lived a lifetime wondering why her father didn't love her. If she and her parents had ever disagreed or been mad at one another, they would've worked it out by the next day. Of course she would want him to patch everything up.

So why'd he have to get mad at her? How could he have yelled at her, Ali Daniels, a girl who'd never fought with anyone? He was an idiot. Cowboy pride, that's what it was. Stubborn cowboy pride.

He should've turned around and run after her, taken her in his arms and told her he was sorry. Instead he'd let her go off, coughing and sputtering. Now he'd have to wait until after her race to talk to her.

The stands were almost full, but he found a spot on the top row and kept his hat low so he wouldn't be recognized. From there he could see his mother and Carl Joseph, still sitting next to Ali's mother. He forced himself to watch the barrel racers instead.

Times for the first five riders were all decent. She would need a great ride to put herself at the top. *Come on, Ali . . . I'm up here, pulling for you. Give it your best.*

The announcer introduced her just as she tore into the arena. Her blonde ponytail flew behind her like pale silk, her trademark black hat and black jeans standing out in stark contrast to her palomino horse.

"Look at her go!" The announcer was excited, keeping the crowd on the edge of their seats. "If she gets this last barrel she could have herself a record-breaker, folks."

Ali flew around the final barrel and blazed back through the gate, but something was wrong. She didn't look right; something in her eyes and the gray color of her skin. Cody stood up, adrenaline flooding his veins. She looked faint, beyond sick. The whole arena had to see that.

"She did it!" The announcer hooted out

loud. "Ali Daniels has the new record, ladies and gentlemen!"

The crowd was on its feet, clapping and cheering for Ali, but Cody climbed on top of the bench and peered over them. He had to see her, needed to know that she was okay. Cody squinted hard, scanning the area where the barrel racers were gathered until he saw her. She was still on Ace, still making her way from the arena. She came to an abrupt stop and then, in a sickening sort of flop, she fell onto the ground.

"Ali!" He tore down the steps, his eyes glued to the place where she lay, motionless. It was his fault; he'd upset her before the race, and now she couldn't breathe. He cursed himself as he took the stairs two at a time. Every step was a frantic plea. *No, not now . . . not yet . . . help her, please. Help her breathe.*

Even from across the stadium he could see people snapping to action around her. Two riders moved in at her side, and a couple of cowboys ran into the arena waving their arms. "Get an ambulance! Hurry!"

A hush fell over the crowd, all eyes trained on the place where Ali had fallen. Cody picked up his pace. Behind him he heard steps and turned to see Ali's mother,

her face pale, eyes wide. "Run, Cody . . . don't wait for me!"

He took off, tearing around the fence toward the competitors' area. Rodeos kept an ambulance on hand. By the time Cody reached the small crowd that had gathered around Ali, the ambulance was just a few yards away.

"Ali!" His voice was lost in the chaos. Emergency personnel were at the center, but there were too many barrel racers and other competitors in the way for him to see what they were doing, whether she was conscious or not.

"Move!" he shouted, and a few people cleared a path. If she needed her inhaler, why hadn't she taken it? What could've made her collapse like that? And why wasn't she getting up?

He had to part his way through the crowd to get to her. By the time he reached the inner circle, they were loading her limp, beautiful body onto a stretcher. Someone was holding an oxygen mask over her face, and through it he saw her blink. She was awake!

"Ali!" He pushed his way to her side and grabbed her hand. "Ali, I'm here." He moved in time with the paramedics, walking beside her toward the ambulance.

She mumbled something and pushed the oxygen away from her face. "Cody . . ." She was pasty gray, her breathing tight and shallow, the way it had been at her ranch that day. "I'm fine . . ." Her words were breathy and weak, barely understandable. "Don't . . . don't worry about me."

"I'm sorry." His heart screamed within him, pounding out a fast and terrible rhythm. *Don't let her die. Please . . .* Why had he gotten her so upset? They were at the ambulance door now; he had only seconds. "I didn't mean it, okay?"

"It's not your fault." She blinked and the movement was slow and fading. "Go ride."

It wasn't his fault? Even now she was thinking of him, reading his mind. Of course it was his fault. He'd gotten her upset; he'd let her walk away coughing when he could've helped her. Whatever happened, he was completely responsible.

Ali's mother ran up. She spoke to the paramedic, and Cody distantly heard him grant her permission to go along for the ride. He shot a look at the other medic, the one closest to him. "Take me, too. She needs me."

"Her mother's going." He lifted the stretcher and slid it into the back of the ambulance. "Only next of kin is allowed; I'm sorry."

"Is she okay?"

The man looked at his partner and then at Ali. "She needs to be seen, but she's stable."

Cody felt himself catch a full breath. "Okay." He met Ali's eyes. "I'll be right behind you. I'm leaving now."

The technician wanted to put the oxygen over her face again, but Ali turned away. "No, Cody. Stay . . ." Sweat drops dotted her face, and the skin around her mouth was still blue. "Ride . . . you can come later. I'll . . . be fine." Her eyes locked on his, and despite the commotion and crowd and frenzied attempts to help her, everything faded away. Everything but her. "I love you, Cody."

Her words were too soft to hear, but he heard them all the same. Heard them to the core of his being. He took a step back, his eyes still on hers. "I love you, too."

Someone closed the ambulance doors and the driver gave three short bursts with the siren, clearing a path through the crowd. And then she was gone. She and her mother, leaving him alone on a patch of dusty rodeo ground, his head spinning. What city were they in, anyway? And what was the name of the hospital? How could he find her if he didn't know where she was?

A bull rider came up beside him and put an arm around him. "They'll take care of her, Cody. Probably just the heat."

The heat? He stared at the guy and opened his mouth to explain that it wasn't the heat; it was her CF. But then he remembered. No one knew, not one of them. Ali looked as healthy as ever. Why would anyone think she was dying of a fatal lung disease? He'd promised Ali he would keep her secret, and even now he wouldn't betray her.

The rider was waiting, but Cody only gave him a quick slap on his shoulder. "Thanks, man. You're right."

Cody didn't know what to do. He started in one direction, stopped and turned around, and stopped again. Why was he at the arena when Ali needed him? He had to find his way to her. The other barrel racers were finishing up now, and the announcer explained that Ali had been taken in for a check.

"Bull riders should report at the judge's table," he said. "That's right, folks, hold on to your hats. We've got the best bull riders on the tour about to take a seat on the rankest bulls around."

Cody had a great draw for the final go-round of the day, and he was third to ride. What was it Ali had told him? Ride first, then come see her, wasn't that it? He paced to the far chain-link fence, grabbed it and stared at the highway beyond. Someone would know where they'd taken her, maybe someone at the announcer's booth.

Riders talked about the adrenaline rush of getting on a bull.

It was nothing to the way he felt now, stomach aching, limbs on fire, head spinning. *Please . . .*

He clenched his fist and drove it into the fence. Fine. If she wanted him to ride, he'd ride. What would eight seconds matter? The paramedic said she was steady, right? He could ride and he'd still be fifteen minutes behind the ambulance. The moment he was finished he'd find out where she was and take her truck. It was unhooked from their trailer; the keys on the floorboard where she always kept them.

In a burst, he turned and jogged toward the chutes. He wasn't stretched out, but that didn't matter. He'd never been more focused in his life. He would ride for Ali, because she wanted him to. After all he'd done wrong that day, the least he could do was turn in a winning performance. He was halfway there when his mother stepped out from the crowd and blocked his path.

"Cody . . ." Fear colored her eyes. "Is she all right?"

A part of him wanted to cry at the sight of her, run to her arms and let her rock away the hurt the way she'd done when he was a little boy. But in the war that was their family existence, she'd chosen sides. He stopped only long enough to nod his head. "She's fine."

He started to move again, but she took hold of his arm. "Let me help, Cody. I'll take you to her."

"No!" He hissed the word. "I can get there myself."

Then he turned and stormed to the area behind the chutes. He grabbed his rope and slipped on his vest. By the time he reached the pen and climbed up the fence, it was his turn. He climbed in, steadied himself over the bull, and dropped onto the beast's back, shoving his mouth guard in place. The animal snorted, pawing the ground. "Not today, mister."

Three cowboys sat on the fence around him, holding on to his vest. Cody wrapped his hand in record time, grabbed the chute with his free hand, and nodded. The ride was wild, twisting him in tight circles and sending him airborne on top of the bull, his arm straight up, legs in perfect position. The bull snorted and Cody felt the spray against his face, smelled the animal's fury.

Not today, bull. Not this cowboy. Cody kept his eyes on the bull's shoulders. Nothing was going to happen to Ali, nothing.

The ride was crazy, more intense than any Cody could remember. Adrenaline filled him, flooding his senses until there was only Cody and the bull, Cody and the ride. Eight seconds passed in a blur, and when the buzzer sounded, Cody jumped off and headed straight for the gates.

He was halfway to Ali's truck when he heard the announcer shout, "Cody Gunner gets a ninety-three, folks; you can live a long time and never see a bull ride like that one! Let's hear it for . . ."

Cody tuned it out.

He climbed into Ali's truck and used her cell phone to call information. There was one hospital in town. Cody phoned for directions as he drove through the parking lot toward the exit. Ten minutes later he walked into the emergency room and spotted her mother.

"How is she?" He was still dirty from the ride. "What's wrong with her?"

"She's okay, Cody. They're giving her oxygen." Her mother squeezed his hand. "Dr. Cleary told her it would get like this."

"But they can make her better, right, get her well again?" He couldn't think, couldn't breathe until he knew she was going to be all right.

"Yes. She'll have to stay in the hospital awhile. Four days, maybe." Ali's mother looked tired. "How'd you ride?"

The matter was so small compared to Ali's health. "Ninety-three." He looked past her, toward the double doors that led to the hospital rooms. "Can I see her?"

Her mother hesitated. "The doctor said only —"

"Ma'am, please." He looked at her again.

She gave a nervous glance at the receptionist's desk. "Okay." She motioned to him. "Stay with me."

They went back and found her in the third room on the right. She was by herself, hooked up to an intravenous bag and oxygen. As soon as he saw her, he felt himself relax. Her color was back. Her mother was right; she was going to get through this. One more time, one more chance.

"Hey, you." He moved to her side.

She looked tired, but she found a smile for him. "Did you stay on?"

"Yeah." He stroked her hair, searched her eyes. "What happened back there?"

"I couldn't get a breath." The weariness lifted. "Did you hear? I set a record!"

"I heard." He bent down and kissed her cheek. He didn't want to talk about their events. "You couldn't breathe? You mean after the race, after holding your breath?"

"Right." She closed her eyes and opened them, more slowly than before. "I'm okay, Cody. They gave me something; I can breathe now."

"It's because you were upset." He ran his fingertips along her brow. "I'm an idiot. I shouldn't have gotten mad."

"No." She swallowed and cleared her throat. "It was the humidity, Cody. Really."

She was wrong, but he wasn't going to push. No sense upsetting her further. "You can breathe okay now?"

"Yes." She put her hand over his. "I'm fine, Cody. Just another tune-up." Concern flashed in her eyes. "You have another ride tonight."

"I can turn out; I don't need this event."

"Cody Gunner!" She placed her hand

over his. "You've never turned out in your life." She looked at her mother, standing a few feet away. "Tell him, Mama. He can't help me sitting here in a hospital room."

Mrs. Daniels came a step closer. "She's right; go ride, Cody."

"I don't need to." He wouldn't take his eyes off her.

"Yes, you do." She closed her eyes, too tired to keep them open. "Go win it."

They talked a few more minutes, until she convinced him she was feeling good, that all she really wanted was a nap. It wasn't until he reached the arena and reported in, that he got the news.

News that made his heart turn somersaults in his chest.

Chapter Sixteen

Night rides always involved the rankest stock, the toughest bulls. It was that way on purpose, designed to bring in the higher-paying crowds and give them a better show. When Cody returned to the arena he got the news he'd been waiting for since he earned his pro card. The bull he'd drawn was none other than the legend, the meanest bull on the tour, a bull so violent and crazed, his owners competed him as often as possible, making a killing off him.

The bull was Chaos.

Of the twenty-three times he'd been ridden in the past two years, Chaos had bucked off twenty-three riders. But that wasn't all. The bull wielded his horns like weapons. In his wake were a trail of broken ribs, concussions, and a spinal injury. On the Pro Rodeo Tour no greater challenge existed than the challenge of riding Chaos. Before Ali, Cody would've paid a year's winnings for a chance on this bull. Just one chance.

But now . . .

Now he carried something inside him that would give Ali another three years. He didn't care if Chaos hurt him; that was part of bull riding. But what if the bull jabbed him in the ribs, what if he punctured his lung, Ali's lung?

His mind reeled.

Should he take the draw, maybe pull off the ride of his life? If he did, it would be the pinnacle of his career, no matter how long he rode. Riding Chaos would guarantee him a win and put him in position to coast into the finals. He paced up and down the alley behind the chutes. Every few minutes he stopped to stretch, thinking about the possibilities.

The smell of burned popcorn and greasy corn dogs filled the air and mixed with the scent of livestock. What should he do? How much of a risk was he willing to take? He refused to scan the stands, afraid his mother was still there. If she was, Carl Joseph would see him this time, and then he'd have no choice but to deal with her, as well. Not that he expected her to come looking. He wasn't even sure she was still there. He didn't care. The only thing on his mind was the wild bull ride ahead, his chance at making history.

And the damage it could do to him if he didn't.

Cody was slated to ride last, and the situation was clear to everyone. Stay eight on Chaos and he'd be first not only at this event, but in the standings. First with no one close behind him.

Still . . . he couldn't get Ali out of his mind. He wore a path behind the chutes, stretching and trying to convince himself it would be okay. Ali would want him to ride, to take his shot at the bull no one could beat. But as he climbed the fence and stared in at the bull, he shuddered.

He already knew what would happen. The bull would fly through the air, bucking him onto the ground and coming back to finish him off. Chaos wasn't content with sending cowboys to the ground; he wanted to kill them. Before Ali, that would've been fine. Let the beast try. He'd ridden unridable bulls before.

But what if he *did* get hurt? What if he had a wreck that damaged his lungs?

He could risk his own life, but not Ali's.

And with that he made his decision. Cody hopped down behind the chutes and headed for the judges' table.

"Gunner, what're you doing?" one of the

cowboys shouted after him. "Your ride's up in a few minutes."

Cody didn't stop. He reached the table and stood in front of the oldest judge in the business, a veteran, pure class and character.

"Cody Gunner?" He gave Cody a curious frown. "You need to be in the chute, young man. How can I help you?"

"I'm turning out, sir." He grabbed his number off the back of his vest and thrust it onto the table. "I can't ride tonight."

"But that's the best draw of the —"

"Thank you, sir."

He didn't say another word until he was at Ali's side.

"I can't believe you turned out." She held his hand and smiled at him. "Everyone's going to think you've lost your edge."

"I don't care." He leaned down and kissed her lips, slow and tender. "As long as I don't lose you." He brushed his nose against hers and drew back a little.

"You won't, Cody. I'm fine."

"Right." He bit his lip. He didn't tell her why he turned out; left her thinking it was his deal, that he couldn't get focused with her in the hospital. He couldn't tell her he wanted to keep his lungs safe. It was better if she didn't know, less upsetting to her.

They talked about the standings, and after a while, her mother came in from the cafeteria. "Your father says hello. He'll call you in the morning."

"Thanks, Mama." Ali gave her a lopsided smile.

They made small talk for half an hour before the doctor came in, a clipboard in his hands, his face dark.

Cody sat on one side of the bed, Ali's mother on the other. He wanted to tell the doctor to leave; they were doing fine without anything else to think about.

"Hello." Mrs. Daniels spoke first. "Have you talked to Dr. Cleary?"

"Yes." The man came to the foot of her mattress and touched her toes. "Hi, Ali. You doing okay?"

"Mmm-hmm." She was breathing easier, but she looked exhausted.

The doctor shifted his look to Ali's mother again. "I ran the test results by Ali's doctor, and, well . . . the news isn't good."

Cody steeled himself. Hadn't he known this was coming? No matter what Ali said about this being another tune-up, they all knew she was getting worse. The coughing, the extra medication, the frantic times when she couldn't breathe. The signs were there for all of them.

"Her functions are bad, right?" Ali's mother took hold of Ali's forearm. "I can tell."

"It's more than her function tests, Mrs. Daniels." The doctor released a heavy breath. "Her lungs are shutting down. She's finished barrel racing."

Ali reached for Cody's hand. She closed her eyes, squeezing his fingers. He wanted to cover her ears, shelter her with his body. Anything to erase what the man had said. This was the day she'd dreaded all her life. She wasn't being given a warning; it was more of a pronouncement.

No more barrel racing. Not ever.

Cody could only imagine the heartache exploding through her, because his heart was breaking, too. She was finished racing? Done with the dream she'd chased since she was eleven? Never again would she race around the barrels, faster than every other rider. She and Ace were finished, finished with the Pro Rodeo Tour, finished traveling around the country, finished climbing the leaderboard.

Ali Daniels would be remembered for blazing onto the barrel-racing scene and staying in the top handful of riders the whole time she competed. But her promise would never be fulfilled; there would be no national championship.

He let his head fall against her hand, willing some of his strength into her. The doctor was going on, saying something about recuperating and using the next few months to get stronger. Then he said something that made Cody sit straight up.

"Dr. Cleary tells me you're planning a lung transplant in December." The man's face was stern, tense.

"Yes." Ali's mother continued to be the spokesperson for the three of them. She hesitated and looked his way. "Cody's one of the donors. Her father's the other."

"That's what I need to talk to you about." The doctor opened the file he was holding. "We rescheduled the transplant for June. Dr. Cleary believes that's as long as we can wait. After consulting with our specialists, I have to agree." He read the file. "Ali would stay a few more days here, and then return home. We'd like her to gain some strength over the next eight weeks, so that she's in the best possible shape for the transplant."

June? Cody froze for a moment, but there was no hesitation. June was perfect. The sooner the better. That made his decision about the season an easy one.

Ali opened her eyes and the three of them stayed silent, the news suffocating them like a desert dust cloud.

"Doctor" — Ali's mother sounded drained, resigned — "could you give us some time to talk?"

"Yes, certainly." He looked from Ali's mother to Ali and finally to Cody. "I wish I could give you some options, but there are none. This is the only plan left."

As soon as the doctor was gone, Ali turned to him. "You don't have to do it, Cody. Someone else could give me a lung; I'm still on the donor list and my case will be more urgent now. June is the worst time for —"

"Ali." He pressed his fingers to her lips. "I'm done with the season."

"No, Cody." Her mother looked at him. "Ali's right. You're at the top of your sport." She clutched the arms of her chair. "You're healthy and whole; if we put her back on the donor list she might get a lung right when she needs it."

"Listen." Cody's tone was calm, convinced. He slid back in his chair. "I'm doing this. Nothing can change my mind. I *want* her to have my lung."

No one said anything. Then Ali reached out and took his fingers. "We could try to wait, Cody. The doctor might be wrong. What's a few months if it'll let you win the championship again?"

"Hear me, Ali. Please." He leaned close and kissed the inside of her wrist. "My season's over whether you have the transplant in June or December. I won't get on another bull until it's over."

"Why? I . . . I don't understand." Her voice was quiet, weak. "I don't need you at home with me, watching me breathe from a machine. I'd rather have you winning rodeos, Cody. Doing what you love."

"I can't." He ran his fingers over her engagement ring and pressed her hand to his face. He didn't want to tell her, but he had to. "I've never worried about getting hurt on a bull, because I only had myself to think about." He shrugged. "I don't know, maybe I wanted the challenge. The pain of a pulled shoulder beat the other pain, the one inside." He found her eyes and held them. "But everything's different now." He sat up and put her hand to his chest. "One of my lungs is already yours, Ali. It's not mine. I'm not worried about myself, I'm worried about the part of me that belongs to you."

Ali's mother covered her face with her fingers. She was crying, doing her best to hide the noise.

Tears filled Ali's eyes, too, spilling down the bridge of her nose onto her pillow. And that's when he knew he'd won. It was time to go home and get Ali well again, time to dream about the days the transplant would buy them. It was possible, wasn't it? A cure could be found while she was living on borrowed time, right?

He leaned over the bed and hugged her. No matter that Ali and her mother were crying, he couldn't bring himself to feel sad. So what if he missed a season of Pro Rodeo? He'd earned plenty of money that year already, and he could always go back when the surgery was behind them.

Ali was going to get better, stronger, and after her transplant anything could happen. She was a survivor, a fighter. If anyone could beat cystic fibrosis, it was Ali Daniels. And now they would be together every day back at her ranch. Ali and her mother were upset now, but Cody could feel nothing but joy over the fact. And then in just a few weeks when she was well enough, they would celebrate the happiest moment of all.

Their wedding day.

Chapter Seventeen

She found the dress at an old boutique in Denver, a small store she and her mother visited on the way back from a meeting with Dr. Cleary. Ali knew the moment she slipped it on. It was perfect, the only dress she could wear to marry Cody Gunner.

It was May, and warm temperatures had come to Colorado. The dress was full-length, layered satin covered with delicate lace, cap sleeves that fell an inch off her shoulders. She tried it on in front of a three-way mirror, and her mother covered her mouth, her eyes dancing.

"Ali, you're a vision." She came up and gave her a sideways hug as they both looked in the mirror. "Remember when I told you how much I hoped and prayed for this?" She turned and faced her. "For you to live long enough to fall in love?"

"Yes, Mama." She angled her head closer to her mother's. "I remember."

"I told you heaven forbid it be Cody."

There was a catch in her voice. "Ali, I was wrong, honey. Cody loves you the way I only dreamed you might be loved."

"I know." She smiled at the reflection of the two of them. "I'm the luckiest girl in the world."

The days passed quickly and a few nights before the wedding, Ali and Cody were outside on the front porch, sitting in the old swing.

"Hey." He looked at her. "I just thought of something; I haven't got your wedding present yet."

"That's okay." She looked out at the winding drive, the one they'd driven down so many times on their way to a rodeo. It was still impossible to believe those days were behind her; it was the hardest part of her new reality. She shifted and caught Cody's eyes. "I don't need a wedding present; you're enough."

"That's not right, Ali. You deserve a wedding present."

She wove her fingers between his and rested her head on his shoulder. A wedding present. She hadn't given the idea much thought, but now that he mentioned it . . . "Okay, tell you what."

"What?"

"After we get married, ride with me out

to the far end of the ranch. Out there I'll tell you what I want."

"In your wedding dress?"

"Yes." She set the swing in motion again. "The minute the ceremony is finished."

He wanted to argue with her, she could see it in his eyes. But he wouldn't. There was too little time to argue over anything now.

The morning of the wedding arrived, bursting with sunshine and new life. Ali went to her bedroom window and looked out. What would it be like to wake up next to Cody, to feel the strength of his body alongside hers? She could hardly wait. If she were smart she would've married him last Christmas when he proposed to her.

A bluebird landed on the tree outside her window. He cocked his head and looked straight at her. Then he hopped three times along the branch and flew off. Something about the bird made Ali think about her sister.

Anna had been her best friend, the sister who was her other half. Together they sat in their safe, clean room with the pastel wallpaper and dreamed of everything they'd do when they got better. Because back then they believed little girls with cystic fibrosis would get better, that one day they could skip across grassy hills and play hide-and-seek around the bushes and craggy rocks and outcroppings of pine trees. That come some autumn afternoon they might ride horses from sunup till sundown without worrying even a bit.

But it hadn't happened. Anna never got the chance to grow up or find her way out of their bedroom or skip across the grassy hillsides or ride horses. Anna should've been there that day. She would've worn pale blue, her favorite color. Her dress would've been long and slender, and she would've placed baby's breath and miniature daisies in her hair. The daisies that grew outside their bedroom window.

She would've loved Cody, loved the way he cared for her and her family. Cody and Anna would've been fast friends, and together with Ali and their mother, the four of them would've played hearts and spades and dreamed of the future.

Ali gripped the windowsill. Tears welled in her heart.

Anna should've been there beside Ali that day, her maid of honor, her best friend. And the fact that she wasn't, that instead she was buried in the cemetery down the road, made Ali mad with a fierceness she'd hidden for a decade. It had been easy to place it all in a box and let it lie there, her sorrow, Anna's death, all of it. Easy to never lift the lid and examine exactly who was to blame, to never even try to make sense of it.

But now . . . now everywhere she looked she saw Anna, and not just Anna, but life and hope and a future full of promise. She'd had a decade of horseback riding and barrel racing, parents who let her follow her dreams, and now the most amazing thing of all.

Cody's love.

Coincidence could explain a lot of situations, but Cody? The fact that his lung was a perfect match for her ailing body? A love that made it hard to know where she ended and he began?

None of it was by chance.

She'd been granted all her dreams but one, and what was a national championship compared to the sweet season she was about to share with Cody? It was a miracle she was even standing there that morning. She could've died her first year on horseback. Dr. Cleary had told them that, hadn't he?

She never should've survived the years she spent on Ace, the friendship she shared with her horse. Ace had taken Anna's place, easing the loss and giving Ali another chance at life. Ace didn't treat her differently for being sick. He didn't take it easy on her or hold back. No, he flew when she was on him, sometimes for whole afternoons before either of them would get tired.

None of that should've been possible.

And then there was her mother's dream. That she live long enough to fall in love, to know the love of a man who cherished her beyond even himself. Who would've thought that Cody Gunner would be that man? But there was Cody, loving her, adoring her, giving himself completely for her.

If he could've taken her disease onto himself, he would've done it. That was the kind of love Cody had for her.

And what about the time out by the back fence, when she couldn't catch her breath? She could've died then, and she never would've known this day, never would've been preparing to stand on a hillside and promise her love to a man whose soul was intertwined with her own.

She'd been spared so much. She drew a breath and smiled. Her lungs would hold up today, she could feel it in her bones. She lifted her eyes to the sky and peered beyond the blue, to the place where her sister must live. As long as she drew breath she wouldn't understand why Anna had to go so young, why she couldn't be here now to celebrate this day with her.

But she couldn't be mad about it, not anymore.

Tears stung at her eyes and she moved closer to the window, the blue sky filling her senses. She sniffed, overcome by a wave of sorrow bigger than the ranch out back. "Can I ask You something?" Her voice cracked, but she kept her eyes toward heaven. "Would You let Anna watch today, please? Give her a front-row seat." Ali closed her eyes. She ached for Anna more today than ever before. "One more thing. Tell her I miss her."

With her parents watching from a few feet away, Ali glided down the stairs. She held a bouquet of red roses, cut that morning from her mother's garden. Cody waited on the landing below in dark jeans, a white button-down shirt, and a wool suit coat. He looked like the prince he would always be.

She didn't have to ask him what he thought of her dress or of how she looked that day. It was written across his face, spilling over from his heart. However long she had left, she would never again look at Cody without seeing his eyes the way they shone as she came to him.

They embraced, Cody's arms strong and protective, one around her waist, one along her upper back. She breathed in the smell of him, his cologne and shampoo and minty breath mixing in a way that was sweetly intoxicating, hinting at all that was to come that day, that night.

Before he released her, he whispered near her ear, "This is the best day of my life."

The pastor and his wife were there also, not far from her parents. The pastor was thick and bearded with a guitar slung over his shoulder. His wife held a camera and a Bible. She took pictures, several of Cody and Ali, others of the two of them with her parents.

Ali pulled the woman aside before the group headed out. There was a song she'd remembered that morning. It was an old hymn, one of her mother's favorites.

"Can you play it for us, at the end, when we're married?" Ali kept her voice low. The song would be a surprise.

"Definitely." The pastor's wife knew Ali's mother. The significance of the song was clear in her expression. "I'd be honored."

"Thank you." Ali found her father then and linked arms with him.

They led the way, with Cody and Ali's mother next, and the pastor and his wife last. The procession took them over freshly mowed grass, past the tomato garden and rosebushes to the bluff, fifty yards from the house. It was a spot made of rock, covered with patchy grass, a place where she and Anna had dreamed of playing when they were little.

Everyone took their places. Cody and Ali in the center, her parents — the attendants — on either side. The pastor adjusted his guitar and tuned it for a few seconds. His wife stood near him and the first song began.

It was one that captured everything about the two of them. It spoke of a dream being like a river, the dreamer like a vessel, and how even when it was impossible to know what was ahead in the journey, the dreamer had no choice but to follow the dream.

A light wind danced across the ranch that afternoon, and wisps of Ali's hair fanned her face. Without turning her head, she studied her father, tall and proud, stoic. He had stood by while she chased her dreams, paying the price of loneliness and uncertainty, but always believing in her. How amazing that his frame was so like Cody's, that they might test so similar in their blood types and compatibility.

The doctors were wrong. She would live far longer than three years with a set of lungs from Cody and her father. They were the strongest men she knew; their lungs would keep her going for a decade at least.

She felt a stirring at her right elbow, and her mother leaned in. Her voice was the softest whisper. "I'm so happy for you, sweetheart."

"Me, too." Ali kept her response low. "It's what you asked for."

"Yes." Their eyes held a moment longer. "Exactly what I asked for."

When the song was over, the pastor opened the Bible and read about love.

"Love is patient and kind . . ."

Ali looked at Cody. The words seemed to be coming straight from his heart to hers, as if what they'd found together was the picture of what love was supposed to be. She handed her bouquet to her mother and took hold of his hands. They had much ahead in the coming weeks, the transplant and a month of recovery. Dangers would always exist for her, but here and now, lost in Cody's eyes, love — the type of love being spoken of now — was all that mattered.

The pastor was finishing the reading.

"Love always protects, always trusts, always hopes, always perseveres." He paused and looked at them. "Love never fails."

It was time for the vows. They'd each written something special and unique, and then together they'd written the last part.

Ali and Cody faced each other, and Cody went first.

"I take you, Ali Daniels, as my wife." He drew a breath and steadied himself. "If I have ten years with you, or a hundred, our time together would never be enough. With you, I'm something I've never been before." He paused. "I'm whole because you complete me. My love for you means I'm no longer sure where I end and you begin." He ran his thumbs along the tops of her hands, his tone steady even as his eyes filled. This last part they'd written together. "Ali, I promise you everything I am, everything I have, as many days as we share together. No matter what tomorrow brings, I will be here. I will stand by you and stay by you. I will be strong when you cannot be strong, and I will hold you up when you cannot stand. My love, my life, is yours, Ali, from this day on."

He slid a delicate white gold band onto her finger and covered her hands with his.

She hesitated, his words still washing over her. Finally she swallowed and found her voice. "I take you, Cody Gunner, as my husband." Everything faded but the man before her and the connection she felt with him. She waited until the lump in her throat relaxed. "I was not looking for love, but you came into my life and brought it. You opened my heart to feelings I'd never known, my eyes to colors I'd never seen. You taught me that love is measured not in years or decades, but in smiles and dreams and shared bits of laughter, in quiet walks and tender embraces and late-night talks." Her voice cracked, but she continued. "Cody, I promise you all of me every day, as many days as we have together. No matter what tomorrow brings" — she touched the place over his heart — "I will be here." Behind her, she could hear her mother sniffling. Tears blurred her own eyes, and she blinked so she could make out his face, his eyes. "I will stand by you in your dreams and stay by you in spirit. I will be strong in heart when you cannot be strong, and I will hold your hand when neither of us can stand. My love, my life, is yours, Cody, from this day on."

She slipped a thicker matching band onto his finger and in the distance she saw a blue jay, just like the one she'd seen that morning. And suddenly she knew her prayer had been answered. Somewhere up in heaven, Anna was cheering for her, cheering and waving her hands and dancing because of what Ali had found with Cody Gunner.

The pastor said a few words about marriage and the commitment it involved. He closed with another reading.

"And now, these three remain: faith, hope, and love. But the greatest of these is love." He paused, his smile lifting the mood. "It is my pleasure to pronounce you husband and wife. Cody, you may kiss your bride."

Again a gentle breeze played in her hair, sending fine wisps of blonde across her cheeks. Cody brushed them back, taking her face in his hands. Then, in a way that mixed delicate tenderness and smoldering passion, he kissed her.

The pastor took a step back and smiled. "Mr. and Mrs. Gunner, I'd like to be the first to congratulate you."

Her parents circled them, hugging them and making the moment last. In the background, the pastor picked up his guitar and started playing. His wife's voice rang full and clear across the place where they stood. The song grew and built and filled Ali's heart with hope and possibility.

Ali caught her mother's eyes. She leaned close and whispered near her ear, "I love you, Mama. I do."

Her mother hugged her, rocking her, the two of them swaying in the breeze. "Everything's going to be okay, honey. Keep believing."

"I will." She drew back and returned to Cody's side. It was time for the part Ali had asked for, the part that made both her parents and Cody nervous. She was supposed to be using these weeks as a time away from horseback riding.

But Ali wanted this, and none of them could refuse her. Not on her wedding day.

She nodded at Cody and smiled. He hesitated, then broke away from the group and headed for the barn. A few minutes later, he galloped out on Ace, cowboy hat in place, headed for Ali. When he reached her, he extended his hand, and with the help of her dad and the preacher, Ali climbed onto Ace and pressed herself snug against Cody's back. She sat sidesaddle, her long dress flowing just past the white lace-up boots she'd chosen for the day.

"You ready?" Cody adjusted his hat, his eyes bright with emotion.

"Ready." She turned and the pastor took their picture. She waved to her parents, and they were off, Cody at the reins.

He took them slow and steady, and she melted into him, enjoying the feel of his body against hers. After several minutes, they were out of sight of the others, and Cody slowed Ace to a stop.

She faced him. "Congratulations, Mr. Gunner."

He tipped his hat to her. "And you, Mrs. Gunner."

"See" — she gave a light giggle — "I was right."

"About what?" He ran his fingers along her spine.

"You *were* chasing me."

"Yes." His eyes caressed her, held her. "And now I'm not letting you go."

The sun was warm against her face, splashing bright rays over a moment that was already brilliant. She worked her hands around his waist and leaned her head on his chest. "I can't believe we're married."

"Me neither." He kissed the top of her head. "Okay, so this is when you tell me what you want for your wedding present, right?"

"Right." She eased herself up, studying him. "Now's the time."

She watched his face, checking for his reaction. Maybe this wasn't a good idea. She didn't want anything to mar the moment, to cast a shadow on their wedding day. Not even something as important as this. She leaned up and kissed him, a kiss that promised more for later when they would drive to the secluded resort in the Rockies, the place where they would spend three nights before coming home and facing the transplant.

He brushed his nose against hers, shading her from the sun with the brim of his hat. "I'm waiting, Mrs. Gunner."

Her smile faded as she found his eyes. "This is serious, okay?"

"Okay." He brushed his knuckles against her cheek, the way he'd done from the first time they kissed. A grin tugged at the corners of his mouth. "I'm very serious."

He wasn't, but he would be. "Okay, this is what I want." She took a slow breath. "I want you to forgive your parents. That's what I want for my wedding present."

She watched her words work their way from his heart to his head and back again. He chuckled, his tone thick with disbelief. "Ali . . ."

"I know you don't want to, but it means so much to me." She took hold of his jacket lapels, hoping her words would breach the walls he'd built in his heart. "I want them on our side, Cody. They're my family now, too."

The muscles in his jaw flexed and for a moment he looked to the side, across the sloped fields and foothills that ran toward the Rockies. Finally he unclenched his jaw and caught her eyes again. "That one . . . might take a while."

"Fine." She kissed the tip of his nose. As long as he was open to the idea, reconciliation was bound to come. A sweet sense of victory flooded her veins, victory and a peace she'd been searching for since that conversation with Cody in the competitors' area the day she had her last barrel race. "Just try. That's all I want."

He searched her eyes. "You know what I want to give you?"

"What?" She put her hands on his knees, steadying herself.

"Time." His lips were tight, his chin strong despite the sudden storm in his

261

eyes. "I want to wake up with you in my arms tomorrow morning and find out that CF was only a bad dream." He ran his fingers lightly down her side. "That you're as healthy on the inside as you look on the outside." He cupped her face in his hands. "I want time to have babies and raise them and grow old with you."

She leaned her shoulder into him and rested her head against his heart. "I want that, too."

They talked for a while longer, about the transplant and her fear that he wouldn't ride again. "You have to, Cody. You have to win another championship." She tugged on his hat. "Win it for me this time, okay?"

He nodded, but his look didn't fool her. It would be a long time before Cody climbed back in the chute with a bull. Not because of a missing lung, but because he didn't want to lose a minute of their time together.

Ali couldn't blame him. As much as she wanted him to ride, she wanted him with her more. They were about to head back home when Ali stopped and turned to him. "I almost forgot your wedding present."

"Mine?" Cody cocked his head. "That's crazy, silly." He lifted her chin, meeting her eyes straight-on. "I have you, that's all I need."

"And something else." Ali gathered the reins and handed them to him. "Here."

"Ali, I don't . . ." Confusion clouded his eyes. "I don't understand."

"I'll still ride him. As long as I can walk I'll ride him." She smiled through her tears. "But after today he's yours, Cody. I'm giving you Ace."

He didn't say anything. Rather, he folded his arms around her and held her for a long time, moving only to pat Ace on the neck now and then. She was giving him Ace? Her most precious possession? Her friend? It was more than Cody could take in.

When they started back toward the house, it was in the silent understanding of all they'd shared that day, all they would share in the days and months to come. There would be pain, yes. But first there would be love. A love that would always protect, always trust, always hope, always persevere.

A love that would never fail.

Chapter Eighteen

The weeks flew by in a blur of unspeakable passion and tender moments, until finally the lung transplant that would stave off Ali's death was only minutes away.

Cody lay on a hospital gurney, prepped and waiting. Ali and her father were ready, too, in separate nearby rooms. The doctor had promised he could see Ali once more before the surgery. Not because he had fears; he didn't. He was convinced the operation would be a complete success. But because he wanted to make sure she wasn't afraid.

The cost became an issue as they neared the transplant date. Ali's parents cashed out the stocks they'd been saving, but they were still short. As soon as he was aware of the situation, Cody paid the difference. Most of his winnings were bankrolled. Other than the cost of riding every week during the season, he didn't need much.

He shifted on the gurney. He had ex-pected to feel the adrenaline, the same sense of heightened alert he experienced whenever he climbed onto the back of a bull — ready to fight for his life. Instead, he was antsy with anticipation, anxious to get the transplant over with.

Ali was much worse now. She couldn't sing or take a walk without getting winded. Even a shower was impossible because the humidity made it too difficult to breathe. The bacterial infection in her lungs wasn't going anywhere; the lung transplant was her only hope.

Cody would've done it back when she first grew worse, but the procedure took time and preparation. Fewer than a hundred live-donor lung transplants were performed each year, most with huge success. Still, the surgery was rare. The right team of doctors at the University of Colorado Hospital in Denver had to be assembled and ready in order for it to be the success they were looking for.

The sun beat on the window of Cody's room, but in the spray of light all he could see was Ali's face, the way she looked the night before when he held her, stroking her hair and memorizing her. It would go well; it had to. They hadn't come this far to run into trouble now. It would be okay for all of them and when transplant and recovery were over, Ali would be stronger, more alive than ever.

He adjusted the sheets and shifted to his side, his back to the door. As he did, he heard someone walk in. Probably another nurse, looking for a sample, ready to poke him with another needle. He turned and what he saw made his stomach drop.

"Hello, Cody . . ." His father shut the door behind him and took a few steps closer. His sleeve was rolled up, and a bandage ran around his elbow. "The doctor told me I could have a few minutes with you."

Cody stared at him, unblinking. How dare his father come now, when he was lying on a gurney, when he couldn't run away, couldn't do anything but face the man? This was a private time between him and Ali and her parents. What would his father know about the sort of love he and Ali shared? Why had he come — and how could his mother have allowed it?

With everything in him, Cody wanted to be mad.

But after a month of being married to Ali, after waking with her in his arms and knowing the intimacy of her touch, it didn't matter how much he wanted to be angry.

He couldn't remember how.

His father took another step. "I'm sorry, Cody." His eyes shifted to the smooth tiled floor. When he looked up again, defeat was written across his face. "You don't have to forgive me; I don't blame you."

Cody blinked and the moment changed. He wasn't in a hospital room a few feet from the father he hadn't talked to in almost fifteen years. He was a boy again, and his father was throwing his things into a yellow cab, walking around to the passenger door and waving good-bye. *This is it, son . . . be good for your mama. This is it* . . . And he was watching his father climb into the cab and shut the door, watching the cab drive off down the street, and he was running after it, as fast and hard as his eight-year-old legs would take him.

And suddenly he thought of something he hadn't thought of in all those years without his father. Why had he run so fast and hard? Why had it mattered so much that he catch the cab, that he stop his father from walking out of his life? The answer came swift and certain, choking his soul and making his eyes blur. The reason was obvious. He ran after him because he loved him, loved his father with an intensity he hadn't known again until Ali Daniels.

Mike Gunner was a pro football player. What little boy wouldn't have thought him bigger than life, a hero who came home and shared a dinner table with them. But Cody's father had been so much more than an image. Back when they were together, Cody was the happiest little boy in Atlanta. He and his father played make-believe football games, and Cody would savor the long afternoons when his dad threw him a ball or tackled him on the living room floor. The sun rose and set on the man because that's how much Cody loved him.

That's why he ran after the cab that day.

For some crazy mixed-up reason, he had blamed his mother for the loss, as if she were at fault for letting him go. But even all of that had been fueled only by the crazy love of a little boy for his daddy. A bond that even hatred couldn't sever. In fact, his hatred for his father was equaled only by the love he'd once felt for him, the love he'd lost. A love that was still alive, because Cody could feel it rushing to the surface, taking away his ability to speak or cry or even breathe.

His father cleared his throat. "I came to say a few things; I might as well get them said." He rubbed the back of his neck, a gesture Cody recognized as his own. Their eyes met and his father's were marked by a vulnerability, an openness that seemed to bare his heart. "I was selfish and wrong when I left you; I couldn't see anything but me." He turned his hands palms up. "It was all my fault, Cody. I couldn't let you . . ." He gestured toward the hospital room. "I couldn't let you go through this without telling you how sorry I am. You and Carl Joseph, you deserved better."

"We . . ." Cody pressed his lips together to keep from crying. "We needed you, Dad."

"I know." Only a few feet separated them, and his father closed the distance. He reached toward Cody with his bandaged arm and held his hand out. "I'm sorry."

Somehow this attempt was different from the time his father showed up at the rodeo. There it felt like a stunt, his way of cashing in on Cody's success and popularity. But here . . . Cody coughed, working out the thickness in his throat. He pointed to the bandage on his father's arm. "What happened?"

He grabbed the spot with his other hand and shrugged. "I gave blood. In case you or Ali or her father need it during the surgery."

Cody blinked, too stunned to move. His father had done what? He'd given blood for them? Not knowing whether Cody would even talk to him, he'd flown to Denver and given blood?

Voices talked in hushed tones in the hallway, and buzzers from a nearby room filled the air. Cody barely noticed. In painful slow motions, the walls in his heart came crumbling down. He still loved his dad, he actually did. No matter how many years the rage had consumed him or how hard he'd tried to battle it into submission. The love was there as long as the little boy in his heart still lived. Tears spilled onto his cheeks. He couldn't speak, couldn't tell his father the things he wanted to say, things that were still awkward. But he did the one thing he could do.

He reached out and took his father's hand.

Ali could breathe again.

This was her first sign that the surgery was over, and that it had gone well. She was still sedated, still not quite awake. But she could breathe. For a long while she lay there, savoring every breath, every sweet, life-giving breath.

The rest of her days she would have a part of Cody inside her, a part of him, and a part of her father. Their gift would give her the chance to think about riding again or having a family or beating CF once and for all. The chance to think about tomorrow and all it might offer. Her father had always been a part of her. But now and forevermore, Cody's life would course through her, giving her strength and hope and time. Giving her a future.

She heard someone walk into the room and come close. "Hello?" Her throat sounded dry, her voice thick and hoarse.

"Ali, sweetheart." It was her mother. The clear, kind voice of her mother. "How are you feeling?"

"Mama . . ." Sleep hung over her, making her eyelids heavy. But she fought to open them. When she did, she squinted, trying to make out her mother's face. "How's Daddy and Cody?"

"They're wonderful, honey." Her mother kissed her cheek. "The surgery was a success for everyone."

Ali closed her eyes, relief adding to the other wonderful feelings awakening throughout her body. But none of them meant anything if she couldn't see him, couldn't be with him. This time she spoke without opening her eyes, her words slow and raspy. "Take me to him, Mama, please. Take me to Cody."

Cody was coming around, trying to open his eyes. The room was quiet, but he had the strangest sense he wasn't alone.

He'd been through a surgery, he remembered that much. His lung was gone by now, gone to Ali, where it belonged. But what had happened before the operation? Had he been dreaming or had his father come by with a bandage on his arm, talking about mistakes and seeking forgiveness?

His head was heavy, groggy from the medication, but he opened his eyes and instantly he had the answers. It wasn't a dream. His father was sitting a few feet away, his head in his hands. Next to him was his mother, and standing near the door was —

"Brother!" Carl Joseph lumbered across the room and shook his hand, too excited to contain himself. "Brother, I'm happy to see you!"

"Thanks, buddy." Cody struggled to bring his hand to his face and massage his brow. "I can tell."

Their parents stood and looked at him. His father took a step forward. "Ali's doing great, son. Her father, too. We've all been praying and . . . the surgery was everything they hoped it would be."

Cody lifted his eyes to his father's. He cared that much? Was he really that different now? In that minute, Ali's request came back to him, the one she'd made on their wedding day. That he might make amends with his parents.

She was right, wasn't she? Life would be better for all of them if forgiveness won out. He'd been given the greatest gift of all — a little more time with Ali Daniels. What right did he have to hold on to anger now, when his whole life was marked by the most amazing sort of love? Life was too short to hate; Ali had taught him that.

"Brother, guess what?" Carl Joseph still had ahold of his hand. He pumped it again. Never mind that Cody had ignored him for the past year, that he'd walked right past him at the last rodeo, the one where Ali had gotten sick. Carl Joseph's love never skipped a beat, never took offense.

"What, buddy?"

Carl Joseph's eyes grew wide. "Dad's here, too. Remember Dad? He's here, brother!"

Their mother took Carl Joseph's hand then and led him back a few steps. Her eyes met Cody's and he saw the fear there, the concern that Cody would break into a fit of rage the way he had before.

Instead, he smiled at her. Then he shifted his gaze and looked at his father, the two of them unblinking. Whatever his father had done before, the man was sorry. He really was. Cody ached for all the years the two of them had missed, the lonely days when, as a boy, he'd needed his dad. But those days were behind them. Here and now he was overcome with a need to be held by the man again, the way he'd been held by him a lifetime ago.

He held out his arms and said the only word he could manage. "Dad . . ."

His father came to him, hugging him so tight it hurt the incisions on his chest. But Cody didn't care. A torrent of sorrow released and Cody wept for all they'd lost, all they might never have found if not for Ali.

And in that moment Cody realized that all those years of bull riding, he'd been kidding himself. The battles he'd fought in the arena had done nothing to ease his hatred for his father, the same way the years had done nothing to ease his need for the man.

Only this could empty him of the rage and bitterness and years of unforgiveness, this embrace that tore at the enemy lines and built a bridge that would take them out of yesterday and into tomorrow.

His dad straightened a bit. "I'm sorry about Ali."

"Me, too." He tried to smile, but his chin was quivering too much. "She's a fighter, Dad. I think the doctors are wrong." He sniffed. "I think she'll get ten more years at least."

"At least." His father hesitated. Then he hugged him again, even tighter than before.

That's when Cody realized his father was crying, shaking as the two stayed locked together. Cody's face was wet, and he wasn't sure if it was from his father's tears or his own. Here, in his father's arms, he was a boy facing the biggest battle of all, the battle for Ali's life. If he was to survive it, he needed all the help he could get. When he could talk, Cody mumbled into his father's shoulder, "I'm afraid, Dad. I can't live without her." He grabbed a couple of quick breaths.

His mother and Carl Joseph joined them, adding their arms to the hug. Cody cleared some space and looked at his mother. "I'm sorry, Mom. I was . . . I treated you awful."

"I always hoped you would find room in your heart for me, Cody."

"Hey!" Carl Joseph jumped a few times.

"That's what we always wanted. That Cody's heart would get better, so he could love people. Even you!"

Everyone laughed, but more tears followed. His mother squeezed in and kissed Cody's forehead. "Yes. Even me."

Cody didn't know where the tears were coming from, but they came like a river. He hugged his mom and then his dad again and finally his brother. The whole time, Carl Joseph patted Cody's knee. "It's okay to cry, brother. Big boys can cry."

They were still like that, his entire family basking in the warmth of forgiveness and new love, when Cody heard Ali's mother's voice in the doorway. He eased the others back again and wiped his hands across his cheeks.

"The nurse said it was okay if you had one more visitor." She stepped inside and behind her, led by two attendants, came a gurney through the door into his room. On the gurney was Ali. Her mother shrugged. "She told the doctor she couldn't get better unless she was with you."

He fought back another wave of tears and held out his hand toward her. "How are you?"

"Listen." She inhaled long and slow and grinned at him. "I can breathe."

He wanted to run from the bed and take her in his arms, but instead he reached out his hand a little farther. Chairs were moved and the room quickly rearranged so that her bed could be placed next to his.

When it was, she slowly reached out and took hold of his fingers. "Well, Cody." She sounded tired, but her expression couldn't have been happier. Her eyes traveled around the room at his mother and father and Carl Joseph, and finally back to Cody. "Wanna tell me about my wedding present?"

He bit his lip, stifling a grin. "Yes, I do." He cleared his throat and looked at the others. "Ali, I'd like to introduce you to my family."

Chapter Nineteen

Their time together passed far too quickly.

The doctors' fears — that Ali's body might reject Cody's lung since he wasn't related to her — never materialized. She took to her new lungs as if they'd always been a part of her. Cody wasn't surprised. He was complete only after she came into his life. It was fitting that a piece of him would complete her, also.

He did his best to convince himself that he hadn't lost a step, that he could run his horse three miles and not hurt for oxygen. But the truth was something a little different. Sometimes after ten minutes in the saddle his chest would hurt and he'd have to slow down some to catch his breath.

Ali's father brought it up just once when he caught up with Cody near the barn. Cody had his hands on his knees, catching his breath.

"Gotta pace yourself now, Cody." He grinned. "We both do."

Everything they'd been told about donating a lung was right on. A little more winded once in a while, but otherwise not much to complain about. Cody didn't talk about it or dwell on it or hardly ever even think about it, and Ali's father was the same way.

All that mattered was Ali.

For two years they lived the type of life most people only dream about and never find. Cody stayed away from bulls and rodeos and anything that might take him from her. They moved into her parents' guesthouse, and he continued on with her father, working the cattle and keeping the ranch in good repair.

Dr. Cleary told Ali from the beginning that, like always, horseback riding would shorten her time. Ali talked it over with Cody, and the two agreed she would still ride. She would have to ride. And so — against medical wisdom — Cody and Ali climbed atop Ace once a day and rode the perimeter of the ranch, galloping across the fields toward the foothills, breathing in the smell of sweet summer grass and gardenias, their bodies moving with the horse in a fluid motion that felt as beautiful as it was to watch.

Cody explained it to Ali's parents this

way: "The doctors want Ali to spend her days trying not to die." Sincerity rang in his tone. "We believe Ali should spend her days trying to live."

Together they found new and breathtaking ways not only to live, but to love.

Because of her new lungs, Ali was strong enough to hike with Cody on easy trails in the Colorado Rockies. Once in a while they would take a picnic to a remote spot and remember their rodeo days.

Ali would recount specific barrel races, the way she felt tearing around the arena on Ace, how she worked so hard to convince everyone she wasn't sick. And Cody would take a half hour to break down an eight-second bull ride, how the rage drove him and how he willed himself to focus the anger into staying on the bull's back.

But like always with Ali, Cody could talk for only so long before he pulled her into his arms and kissed her, savoring her, loving her the way he'd promised to love her on their wedding day. And sometimes, during those remote mountainside picnics, their bodies would come together and — without climbing another step — they would discover heights they hadn't imagined possible.

One early fall afternoon they rode Ace to

the small nearby cemetery where Anna was buried. They climbed off the horse, joined hands, and stood above the marker. *Anna Daniels, 1976 to 1986. Beloved daughter. Sister. Friend.*

Reds and yellows screamed from the surrounding trees, summer's last desperate show of life, but the two of them were silent. What could they say about a ten-year-old girl who'd lost her life? Whose living was over before it really began?

Cody read the inscription again. "I wish I'd known her."

"Yes." Ali bent down and brushed dirt off the corner of the stone. "I wish that, too. You would have liked her."

Ali had talked about Anna before, how she would've laughed when Cody told one of his tired jokes or how she might've been a rodeo queen if she'd had the chance or how she would've enjoyed a certain brilliant sunset. But that day, staring at Anna's tombstone, Ali leaned her back against Cody's chest and brought his arms around her waist.

"Marry again, Cody. Promise me."

Fear grabbed hold of every muscle, and his chest stiffened. "Actually" — he kept his tone casual — "I believe bigamy's still against the law."

"Cody, please." She let her head fall back against his shoulder, her eyes toward the sky. "You know what I mean." Jasmine bushes were scattered throughout the cemetery and the air was sweet with the smell. She tapped the heel of her boot against the toe of his. "After I'm gone I want you to fall in love and get married again." She turned her head and found his eyes. "I want you to have children."

"Don't, Ali." Sorrow and dread and anger took turns punching him in the gut, but anger came out on top. "I want kids with you."

She turned the rest of the way and looped her arms around his neck. "I want kids with you, too. They told us in March, remember? I can't have them — you know that."

"There has to be a way." He hated having no options. "Let's talk to Dr. Cleary again."

"There's no way, Cody. That's why I want you to promise me."

He narrowed his eyes, fighting back angry tears. "Please, Ali . . ."

"It's all right to talk about it." Her voice was softer than the breeze. "When I go, you'll be too young to live the rest of your life alone."

"No." He pressed his face against hers, and his hands moved up from her waist to her lower back. He couldn't be angry when she was so alive, when his life was so full of her. "You're forgetting something."

"What?" She leaned into him.

"You've got my lung in that body of yours." He touched the back of her neck, making slow circles beneath her hair. "Gunner lungs last longer."

"Is that right?"

"Yes." He kissed her throat and nuzzled his face against hers. "So there."

He thought about what he'd said. It was true; he was strong and in good shape, and so was her father. Maybe the doctors were wrong; maybe with the right lungs, a transplant would give her twenty or thirty years.

Maybe someone would find a cure for cystic fibrosis.

She angled her head, her eyes a mix of patient love and determination. "I still want you to marry again."

He took a step back and put his hands on her shoulders. "You know what I'm going to do?"

"What?" She looked past his jumbled emotions, straight to his soul.

"When we celebrate our fortieth anniversary, I'm going to remind you of this conversation." He raised an eyebrow. "Then you'll feel pretty silly, huh?"

"Yes." Her eyes danced and a smile lit her face. "Pretty silly."

"Okay, then. That's what I think about your request."

She tucked her chin against her chest, her expression as sweet as it was coy. "Can we make a deal?"

He sighed and placed his fingers along her cheekbones. "You're pretty demanding for a woman."

"I know." She grinned. "It's my nature."

"But . . . since I'm a cowboy and it's a cowboy's nature to be a gentleman, what's the deal?"

"Okay." She bit her lip. "Here it is: If I go before you, you'll get married again and —"

He shook his head. "I told you —"

"Wait . . ." She held a finger to his lips. "Let me finish. If I go before you, you'll get married again. And if you go first . . . I'll remarry." She lifted her eyebrows. "How's that?"

His jaw hung open in mock surprise and he mouthed the word, *You?* He took a step back, desperate to keep things light. "You'd remarry?"

She poked her fingers at him and giggled. "Come on, Cody; I'm serious."

The humor left him. He stared at her, not sure what to say. "I can't, Ali."

"You can't?" Disappointment shaded her face. "You can't remarry?"

"No." He didn't blink, couldn't pull himself from her. "I can't believe you'll ever be gone."

There were other times.

Times when she'd have a checkup with Dr. Cleary and get glowing reports on her lung function tests and bacteria counts, and Cody would believe every lie he'd ever told himself. She wasn't going to die; she was fine, cured, a new person. The disease didn't stand a chance against a competitor like Ali Daniels. The lies helped him sleep at night, but they couldn't stop the passing of days. One after another they came, and each one as it left took with it a small piece of Ali's good health.

The end crept up on them like the last scene in a favorite movie.

Diabetes set in, and Ali's kidney functions fell. Always the fear was a bacterial infection. With cystic fibrosis, some infections could be fought with IV antibiotics. Others would settle in and chip away, taking ground one day at a time until a person's body simply gave up. The pancreas and her digestive system, even her kidneys, could hold their own for years with such an infection. But once a resistant bacteria moved into her new lungs, it would be only a matter of time.

The first pneumonia came just after their third Christmas.

Ali went to bed with a sore throat and an ache in her chest. She woke up coughing as hard as she had before the transplant. Cody thought about running into the main house for a thermometer, but there was no need. She was burning up. He helped her dress, bundled her in blankets, and carried her through a thick layer of snow to her parents' house.

The four of them went together, Ali's father driving, her mother in the passenger seat. Cody sat in the backseat cuddling Ali, stroking her head and telling her to hold on, she'd be well again in no time.

At first it seemed he was right.

Dr. Cleary put Ali on oxygen and gave her high doses of intravenous antibiotics and fluids. Four days later she seemed as healthy as she had before getting sick, with one exception. She was tired.

"We'd expect you to be tired, Ali. But really" — the doctor raised an eyebrow, imploring her — "stay off the horse for a while. A month or two, at least."

Ali looked at Cody, and he saw something in her eyes he'd never seen before. He saw fear. For as long as he'd known her, no matter what illness she faced, even before receiving the new lungs, Ali never looked scared.

But now she was on her last chance.

No lung transplant loomed in the distance for her this time. Rather, if her lungs didn't respond to treatment, if she didn't take it easy and build her strength back, she might never get better.

This time Cody and Ali agreed she should follow the doctor's orders — at least until she recovered and her tests were back to where they'd been. It was winter, so Ali wouldn't miss being on Ace the way she would've any other time of the year. The weeks drifted by; Cody worked less and whenever he wasn't working, he was with her.

They watched old movies — *Casablanca* and *Gone With the Wind* and *An Affair to Remember* — and they spent hours playing backgammon and reading out loud together. Reading was a surprise delight for Ali. All her life she'd stayed away from books, not wanting to waste a single day when she could be outside living.

But books were marvelous now, opening doors to wonder and mystery and magical places Ali had never imagined existed. Her favorites were *The Adventures of Tom Sawyer* and *The Chronicles of Narnia*. Ali loved *The Last Battle*, the final book in the Narnia series.

"Listen again, Cody." She would turn to that part of the book, her voice thick with tenderness. " 'All their life in this world and all their adventures in Narnia had only been the cover and the title page.' " She would stop, take a breath, and continue. " 'Now at last they were beginning Chapter One of the Great Story which no one on earth has read: which goes on forever: in which every chapter is better than the one before.' "

For a moment she would fall silent, staring at the page. Then she would look up, tears in her eyes. "That's how heaven will be, right?"

Cody would draw her near and kiss her cheek, absorbed in her. "Yes." He would search her eyes. "But not for a long time."

She would only smile and take his hand, switching the conversation to Tom Sawyer and the marvels of childhood magic and making memories along the banks of the Mississippi.

Lazy winter days made for early nights, and often Ali was tired. But Cody would argue the fact whenever Ali's parents brought it up.

"I'd like to see more color in her cheeks." Her mother would pull Cody aside every week or so, a frown knit into the lines on her face. "She doesn't look right."

And Cody would find his most confident tone, his most relaxed smile. "It's winter." He'd pat Ali's mother on the shoulder. "Anyone would be pale after a season indoors. Wait till spring; she'll have more energy then."

But by late March, she didn't have more energy; she had a second bout of pneumonia. After another week in the hospital, Dr. Cleary was reluctant to send her home.

"I'd like to keep you here; I think the IV and oxygen tent would help some."

"But not a lot?" Cody was confused. He stood near the head of Ali's bed. He looked at her parents and then at her and finally back to the doctor. "The hospital's always been a good thing for her."

The doctor frowned. It took a moment

before he looked up. "In the past we could get her better."

"Meaning?" Ali took hold of Cody's hand, her eyes on Dr. Cleary.

A sad-sounding sigh left the man's lips. "It's not good, Ali; your lung function's way down and" — he breathed in slowly through his nose — "we can't treat the bacteria." He sat on the edge of her bed and took hold of her right foot, his eyes damp. "I'm afraid it's in both lungs."

And like that, the end was introduced.

Cody felt strange and disconnected.

He wasn't in the room standing next to Ali's hospital bed. He was on a grassy bluff at her parents' ranch, looking into her eyes, knowing she had never looked more beautiful, more whole and well. And he was taking her hand and placing a ring on her finger and promising to be strong when she could not.

Only how could he be strong now? The doctor was basically telling them she wouldn't get better. Her hand was still in his, and he squeezed it. *Cowboy up, Gunner. Cowboy up.*

He locked his jaw and blinked hard. *Get me through this.*

The room had been silent, the news

working its way through the room, through their hearts and minds like a slow, deadly fog.

"So . . ." Ali's eyes showed no reaction. She coughed twice, rib-jarring coughs, and stared at the doctor. "How long do I have?"

"It depends." He folded his arms tight. "A month, two maybe. Stay indoors, away from your horse, maybe a little longer."

"But if she stays in the hospital, wouldn't that . . ." Cody couldn't finish, couldn't bring himself to have this discussion. Talking about it would make it true, and it wasn't true; it couldn't be true. Anyone could get pneumonia, right? It didn't mean it was the end.

The doctor was biting his lip. "If it would make a difference, I'd keep her for a month." He gave a defeated shake of his head. "At this point, I think she'd be happier at home."

Ali pulled Cody's hand close and pressed it to her cheek. Her eyes stayed on the doctor. "How will I know? Will there . . . will there be a sign?"

"It'll get harder to breathe. Harder every day." He angled his head, his expression as honest as it was anguished. "You'll know, Ali."

Three days later, they brought Ali back to the ranch, and the doctor was right. Her breathing grew worse, labored by heavy bouts of coughing that nothing could touch. Not her compression vest or medication or even the prayers Cody and her parents uttered constantly on her behalf.

Cody took to sleeping light, in case she needed him. A glass of water, a cold cloth, or the comfort of his arms around her. One morning, Cody was half asleep when he felt her hand on his shoulder.

"Cody?" She was wheezing, her breathing shallow. "Wake up."

"What?" His eyes were open before she finished his name. He sat up, his heart pounding in his throat.

She met his eyes, the intensity between them so deep, so strong it hurt. "Take me out on Ace." A smile just barely lifted the corners of her mouth. "Please."

Cody hesitated. He wanted to tell her no, she was in no shape to go outdoors, let alone on a horse. But he couldn't. This determination, the will to live no matter the cost, it was part of what he loved about her.

"Okay." He took her hand, helped her to her feet, and found two sweatshirts for her. She was thinner than she'd ever been, and cold most of the time. Some days she wore multiple layers and a jacket. But the air had warmed over the past week, so two should be enough.

Together, without saying anything, they headed for the barn.

Rain would've fit the feelings in Cody's heart, but the morning was clear. Sunshine splashed across the bluest sky of spring and only a few puffy clouds hovered near the distant mountains. Leaves were unfurling from the branches of the oak trees, and clumps of grass grew thick and bright green at the base of the pines on the north side of the house. Everywhere, new life was springing up across the ranch.

Everywhere except in Ali.

Cody kept his arm around her as they walked, protecting her, letting her determine the pace. He was horrified at the changes in her from the day before. She was slower, her steps shaky, a pasty gray had taken over her complexion. And the rattling in her chest didn't go away no matter how often she stopped to cough.

Fear tried to push its way between them, but Cody refused it. If Ali wanted this, he would give it to her. And with everything in him he would pretend things were different, that they were heading out for a ride because the bright spring morning demanded it.

They were almost to the barn doors when Ali turned to him. "Thanks, Cody. This means a lot."

He smiled at her because he couldn't talk.

Once inside, Ace looked up and whinnied, soft and curious. Cody had been taking care of him, riding him when Ali slept in the afternoon. But this was the first time she'd seen him since just after Christmas. When they were a few feet away, Cody let her take the lead.

"Hey, Ace." Ali pushed herself, her pace stronger than before. She opened the gate, and when she was inside she put her arms around his neck.

The horse responded, softer this time. He turned his head, brushing his chin against the side of her face.

She rested her head against his mane. "Ace . . . I missed you, boy."

Cody's throat was so thick, he could barely breathe. This was the horse Ali had raised from birth, the one she had broken and trained and taken across the country three times over. Ali had once told him that Ace understood things a horse shouldn't understand. When it was a big rodeo, when a championship or high-stake prize money was up for grabs, Ace would sense her excitement and give her a ride equal to the task. Likewise, he sensed when she was sick and responded with a gentler ride.

Watching now, Cody knew it was true.

There were tears in her eyes when she turned to him. "Ready?"

He gave a short nod and went to work. Once Ace was saddled, Cody climbed on and helped her up in front of him, the way he'd done so many times before. Often when they'd ride around the ranch together, he'd hold the reins by putting his arms around her waist. But this time he handed them to her.

Ali set out at a trot, but as she left the area around the corral, she broke into a run. Not the all-out record-breaking run she and Ace were capable of, but a gentle run that mixed grace and strength and restraint with every stride. He held tight to her, willing her to breathe, to survive this ride without anything worse happening.

It took only a few minutes to realize where she was going. She was taking Ace on the familiar route, the one around the perimeter of the ranch. Cody's heart kept time with the pounding rhythm of the horse's hooves. What if Ali couldn't catch her breath? What if she fainted, too far from the house to get help? Why had he agreed to the ride without telling her parents where they were going?

Halfway around — near the back fence — she brought Ace to a stop and fell back against his chest. "Ali?" He took hold of her shoulders and leaned his face in close. "Are you okay?"

"Yes." Her breathing was hard and fast, but it wasn't raspy like it had been back at the barn. "I feel wonderful."

The tension in his muscles eased some. "Can you breathe? Maybe we should get back just in case you —"

"Cody." She angled herself so she could see him. "I'm fine." She pressed her shoulder into him, and turned Ace so she could see back across the expanse of her parents' ranch. "The day after Anna's funeral, I sat in my bedroom alone. Nothing felt right, so I walked to the window and looked out at all the grassy meadows and bushes, beyond our ranch to the neighbor's farm."

He pictured the scene, studying her so he wouldn't miss a word.

"The neighbor had a palomino horse; every day Anna used to dream of riding him. Only she never got the chance." Ali lifted her eyes to an evergreen a few feet away. "So that day I snuck out of the house and ran through the grass and past the bushes." There was a smile in her voice. "And I knew, I just knew Anna was watching me."

He waited, his fingertips light along her outside arm.

"From the moment I stood next to that horse, I was sure I'd never go back indoors." She smiled up at him. "Except to sleep."

"You're a fighter." He kissed the top of her head.

"I told myself no matter what happened I'd have no regrets." She looked at him again. "But I was wrong."

He shook his head. "No, Ali."

"Yes." Her eyes held his. "My only regret is that maybe . . ." Her voice cracked. She brought her hand to her throat and hesitated. "Maybe if I'd stayed inside more, I could've had more time with you."

"Ali . . ."

"I just wanted you to know that." She sat up a little straighter. The familiar wheezing was there, but it was better than it had been in days. She held his eyes with hers. "Every time you ride Ace, every time you look at him, I want you to see me, Cody. I want you to remember how every day with you was a gift. You . . ." She swallowed, her voice tight. "If you hadn't chased me, I never would've caught you."

"Oh, I see." Cody leaned his chin on top of her head, his tone easy. "You caught *me*, is that it?"

"I was keeping it a secret." She giggled, but the effort led to a short bout of coughing. When she caught her breath she folded her hands around his. "This is my last time out, Cody. The doctor was right."

Cody's heart beat faster. "Ali, please." He shook his head. "Don't say that."

"It is." She drew a long breath, one that made her wince. "The doctor said I'd know, and I do. I knew this morning."

Tears blurred Cody's vision and he blinked hard. Was she right? Was this the last time Ali Daniels would sit on a horse, the blazing Ali Daniels? He remembered her question. "I'll always see you, Ali." He snuggled closer to her. "How could I see Ace and not see you?"

She smiled. "My mama always said we looked alike, me and Ace. I guess it's the blonde hair."

They were quiet for a while. Cody willed his anxious soul to settle down, but it wasn't listening. He couldn't get the thought out of his mind. What if she was right? What if this really was her last ride? The possibility made him crazy with fear.

After a few minutes, Ali took hold of the reins. "Ready?"

"No." He wanted to scream at the heavens, jump off Ace, and run until he couldn't take another step. No. A million times no. He would never be ready to leave their private shared world of horses and open ranchland and April blue sky. He couldn't believe for a minute that this was the last time he and Ali would ride together, the last time he would feel her body against his as they pounded out an ageless rhythm across the fields.

"Cody?" She looked over her shoulder at him. Her breathing was getting worse.

"Okay." He pressed his cheek against hers and closed his eyes.

The whole way back he kept his arms around her waist, his eyes shut, memorizing the feel of her as her back brushed against his chest, the sensation of her silky blonde hair dusting his cheeks.

Just before they turned into the barn, she pulled to a stop. Ace must've sensed she was in trouble, because he lifted his head, offering her his neck to lean against.

She smoothed his blonde mane and patted the side of his head. "Attaboy, Ace."

She turned to Cody. "I read something the other day."

He moved his hands up from her waist, running his fingers along her arms again. "Hmmm?"

She looked away and coughed twice. "It was a quote from some guy." A hawk circled overhead and she raised her eyes toward it. "He's dead now."

"Too bad." Cody kept his voice even. He hated talking about death. "What's the quote?"

"Before he died, he told people, 'Soon you will read in the newspaper that I am dead. Don't believe it for a moment. I will be more alive than ever before.'" She looked at him, beyond his confident facade to the terrified places of his soul. "That's what I want you to say about me, okay, Cody? Tell everyone."

"Ali . . ." He placed his hand on her cheek and cradled her head against his chest. If only she could stay this way, safe in his arms.

"I mean it." She covered his fingers with hers. "It won't be long. Tell them I'm not dead, I'm alive." She hesitated and when she talked again there was a smile in her voice. "Tell them I'm riding with Anna, chasing her across the fields and playing hide-and-seek in the bushes. Okay, Cody?"

"Do you . . ." He didn't want to say the words. "Do you really think it's soon?"

"Yes." She coughed again, and the struggle was back with every breath. "Will you tell them?"

He turned himself toward her, framed her face with his hands and kissed her, a kiss that willed life into her, one that wanted her to be wrong about the timing. But he wouldn't keep her waiting, not for another moment. He pulled back and searched her eyes. "I'll tell them."

"Thank you, Cody." She pulled the reins to one side and headed into the barn.

He climbed off first and then helped her down. She walked around and stood in front of Ace, the horse she'd ridden and counted on and competed with for a decade. Ace, who for years had been her only friend.

For a long time she stared at her horse. Then she leaned in, looped her arms around his neck and kissed him on the bridge of his nose. "Be good, Ace."

With a single step, she turned to Cody and fell into his arms. Her tears came then, waves of them. Wrapped in his embrace, she shook, ripped apart by a sorrow that knew no limits.

He rubbed her back, and when she had control again, she looked up. "I'm not sad."

A half smile raised his lips. "I can tell."

She made a sound, but it was more cry than laugh. She brought her fingers to her mouth and shook her head. "What I mean is, I didn't sit in a room and watch life through a window." She held on to his shoulders and kissed him. "I didn't win a national championship, but I did everything else I ever dreamed of doing. And now . . . I'm not afraid." She smiled, her eyes warming him to the core. "I just wish" — her voice caught and she waited a beat — "I just wish I could take you with me."

"Oh, Ali . . ." He forced himself to find his voice. "Me, too."

Once more she glanced over her shoulder at Ace. Then she turned and held out her hand. "Take me in."

She didn't look back again after that.

Not when they left the barn or when they headed into her parents' house through the back door. From the moment she was inside, her breathing grew worse, more strained with every passing hour.

None of the usual methods brought her relief.

Her decline was swift and sure, and she slept through much of it.

By that evening, Cody was convinced. The ride earlier that day, their conversation, all of it had been a miracle, nothing less. Ali might not get better, but they'd been given one single, spectacular morning, a morning that would forever cast light on the broken places of his heart.

Dr. Cleary was contacted, but he gave Ali a choice. She could come to the hospital and have a few more days. Or she could stay home with her family. Ali chose to stay home. The days blurred, Ali fighting her disease the way she'd always fought it, with rolled up sleeves and gloves off.

"I'm trying to hold on, Cody," she told him one night as he lay beside her, studying her. "I'm still trying."

"I know." He ran his fingers through her hair, willing life into her, believing that somehow, someway, they still had a chance. "Don't ever stop; there's still a chance."

Ali smiled. "That's what . . . I love about you." She swallowed, every word a breathless struggle. "You never stop . . . believing in me."

"No, baby, never." He leaned in and brought his lips to hers. "You can do anything."

"Hold me."

He worked his hands beneath her shoulder blades and hugged her lightly. Any pressure on her chest would make it harder for her to breathe. "Stay with me, Ali."

"I will." She pressed her face to his. "I'll just . . . never let go."

She lived two days longer than Dr. Cleary thought possible, clinging to Cody and life, and promising to never stop.

But in the end it wasn't enough.

On a clear late-April day, two weeks after their morning ride, Ali died in his arms.

For a long time — after her parents left the room and after someone had been called to come for her body — Cody held her, clinging to her, breathing in the smell of shampoo still fresh in her hair.

The media learned the story overnight. Hundreds of cowboys and barrel racers and organizers from the Pro Rodeo community attended the funeral. Ali Daniels was no longer a mystery, and they were collectively stunned at the truth, rallying together in their support of Cody and her family.

Cody's parents and Carl Joseph flew in, too, surrounding Cody with a sort of love he had craved all his life.

Carl Joseph came up to him before the service. "Brother." His lower lip quivered. "I'm sorry about Ali."

"Thanks, buddy." Cody crooked his arm around his younger brother and hugged him hard, rocking back and forth.

"She was a good horse rider." Carl Joseph pulled back, his brow furrowed, sincerity and sorrow written in the lines of his face. He raised his hand and pointed to the sky. "Up there, you know what I hope?"

"What?" Cody still had one hand on his brother's shoulder.

"I hope God gives her a horse."

Cody closed his eyes and he could see Ali and Ace, running like the wind together, blazing a trail across the fields behind her house. He opened his eyes. "Me, too, buddy." His throat ached from the sadness. "Me, too."

Ali was everywhere that day.

She was in the eyes of her mother, quiet and stoic, mindless of the tears that streamed down her face. She in the strength of her father, as he placed a bouquet of daisies on her coffin. And she was with Cody, also. In the way he took the microphone and talked about Ali, her determination and grace.

"Ali wanted me to tell you something." He looked at the crowd of familiar faces. "You think she's dead, but don't believe it." Her voice played in his mind. "She is more alive now than ever before."

She was there when he returned to his seat and took his mother's hand, and again in the long hug he shared with his father.

Cody thought it fitting.

Ali had taught him to love; and now that love would be her legacy.

But she never taught him how to let go.

And when the funeral was over, when his parents and Carl Joseph boarded a plane and headed back home to Atlanta, something happened that Cody didn't expect.

The old anger came back.

Or maybe it wasn't the old anger, but a new, unfamiliar anger, a feeling of rage and helplessness and a strange sort of not knowing. Not knowing what to do or where to go or why he should climb out of bed or how he was ever supposed to feel right again.

Whatever it was, habit suggested he keep it inside.

He stayed the summer at her parents' ranch, most of it on the back of Ace. Out on the ranch, missing her, doubts peppered him like springtime hail. Why wasn't she allowed to live? Heaven would have her for eternity; all he'd wanted was a few decades.

And why hadn't she won the national championship? Strange, but some days that bothered Cody most of all. One barrel? One lousy barrel had made the difference? It wasn't right.

"Cody, we're all missing her," her mother would say every few days. "If you want to talk, I'm here."

Every hour made the strange feelings inside him clearer, more intense. Finally he figured it out. The pain wasn't anger at all; it was sorrow. A sorrow with fingers that sometimes squeezed his soul, creating an ache that spread from his chest to his shoulders and knees and feet. Other times sorrow was an ocean, deep and wide and vast, and he a lone swimmer, drowning, without any hope of reaching the shore.

Sorrow was a lot like anger.

He could hide it from people, but it was there when he woke up, and when he closed his eyes at night. And nothing, not the act of saddling Ace or tending the cattle or fixing fences or talking to Ali's mother, made it any better. Cody Gunner knew only one way to deal with the pain.

By the sixth month he made up his mind.

He contacted the PRCA and, given the circumstances, permission was granted. Another rider gave him a room at his ranch in California where Cody practiced two months straight. That January in Denver, when the season started, Cody took a seat on his first competitive bull in three seasons. By then he had a reason, an intensity, a battle even greater than the one he'd waged against anger or disease.

This time the dragon that needed slaying was sorrow, a sorrow that would kill him if he didn't fight it. With every amazing bull ride that season, he battled the sadness, the aching way he missed her. And with every ride he could feel her there, beside him. In him. He didn't fly from one rodeo to the next the way he used to. This time he bought a trailer like Ali's, and parked it in familiar places adjacent to the rodeos. Places where he and Ali had first found each other, places where he could sit outside and remember.

The season was a wild and reckless one, taking on bulls with a confidence that defied understanding. People in Pro Rodeo circles wondered if grief had made Cody Gunner crazy, getting on the back of a bull when his body held just one lung. A single jab of a bull's horn and he wouldn't make it out of the arena.

Cody didn't care. The season was something he had to do, had to experience, and in December he stood in the winner's circle, the national champion a third time.

A few days later he flew back to Colorado to get his things and tell Ali's parents good-bye. His family was in Atlanta; he wanted to be there, too. That week, one afternoon he found Ali's mother in the garden and handed her his championship buckle.

"It belongs to you," he told her.

And it did. Because without Ali, without knowing her and loving her and missing her with an intensity stronger than any bucking bull, he would never have competed. He certainly never would've won. So the buckle belonged to her family — it was the one Ali had always wanted.

The season served its purpose.

Along the way Cody learned the truth about sorrow, and that was this: it would never leave. And so he did what Ali would've done. He took a deep breath, held it, and rushed full on toward it. He embraced it and entertained it, and finally he made peace with it.

Epilogue

Cody opened a horse farm on a ranch outside Atlanta, and a year later his parents and Carl Joseph moved onto an adjacent piece of land. Some days, on warm evenings when Ace was in the pasture, Cody would squint from the back porch of his house, and always he would hear her voice.

Every time you ride Ace, every time you look at him, I want you to see me . . .

And he did, but not the way she had looked that last morning, thin and pale, breathing good-byes. Rather, he saw her alive and well and holding her breath, strong in the saddle, flying around a cloverleaf of barrels.

The way he would always see her.

Now that the rodeo world knew Ali's story, Cody had no choice but to leave everything about her competitive years to the ages, a story that would be told again and again as young riders came up through the ranks. But the real story, who Ali was away from rodeo, would always belong to only a handful of people, the way she had belonged to a handful of people.

And most of all, she would belong to him.

His favorite photo of Ali was taken on their wedding day. She was smiling, wearing her long white dress, daisies in her hair, eyes shining, convinced she would beat cystic fibrosis, that the bond between the two of them was stronger than medicine or disease or even time.

Whenever Cody stopped and looked at the picture, he was convinced of the same thing. Though she'd been wrong about beating the disease, she was right about one thing: The bond between them would remain until his dying day.

Flesh had failed Ali Daniels. But love never did; it never would. No matter how far the years took him from Ali's life, her love would live on.

Because it lived on in him.

Author's Note

This story was inspired by the hundred or so people each year who donate a lung to someone they love, someone with cystic fibrosis. All for the chance to buy a little time, maybe a thousand tomorrows, maybe a few more or less.

Ali Daniels' experience with CF was individual to her, the way the disease is to each person who has it. Her situation was not intended to illustrate an average case or average limitations. I tried to keep her situation within the realms of possibility and reality.

Exercise is encouraged for people with cystic fibrosis, but not in a place with allergens and irritants that might harm the lungs. My research showed that it would be highly unusual for a person with CF to run barrels on the Pro Rodeo circuit. But determination and will made Ali Daniels special.

I chose to write about CF because of a

little boy named Matt who has the disease. He plays basketball on my husband's fourth-grade team. For Matt, there's no talk about his future in the sport. No worries about potential scholarships down the road. These *are* the good old days for Matt. He plays today because he loves it. He plays like an all-star, with his entire heart. In the same spirit that Ali Daniels rode horses.

In 1970 a child born with CF was expected to live only to age ten. That number has risen to a life expectancy today of thirty-two years. If you're interested in volunteering or helping out the Cystic Fibrosis Foundation, you can contact them at www.CFF.org. Their motto is *"Adding tomorrows every day."*

In addition, though I set this story within the context of a real Professional Rodeo Cowboys Association tour, the characters are completely fictional. Any similarities to real characters or events are entirely coincidental and unintentional. I received a great deal of help from professional cowboys and rodeo organizers in researching this book. Errors in accuracy are mine.

A Thousand Tomorrows is about the sort of love that is patient and kind, a love that always protects, always trusts, always hopes, always perseveres. A love that never fails. Cody and Ali showed us that love is not the way around our problems. It is the way *through* them. Remember, when all things have passed away, these three remain: faith, hope, and love. But the greatest of these is love.

You can find out about my other books or our family's adoption story or my Red Gloves Christmas series by visiting my website, www.KarenKingsbury.com. Sign up for my newsletter, and I'll update you every month or so about new books or speaking events. Drop me a note at my guestbook or by emailing me at rtnbykk@ aol.com.

May God bless you and yours . . . until next time,

Karen Kingsbury

About the Author

Karen Kingsbury is America's favorite inspirational storyteller. She is the author of the #1 bestselling *Reunion* and more than thirty other emotionally gripping novels, many of which have been adapted for film and television. Previously a staff writer for the *Los Angeles Times* and a *People* magazine contributor, Karen lives with her husband and six children in the Pacific Northwest.

The employees of Thorndike Press hope you have enjoyed this Large Print book. All our Thorndike and Wheeler Large Print titles are designed for easy reading, and all our books are made to last. Other Thorndike Press Large Print books are available at your library, through selected bookstores, or directly from us.

For information about titles, please call:

(800) 223-1244

or visit our Web site at:

www.gale.com/thorndike
www.gale.com/wheeler

To share your comments, please write:

Publisher
Thorndike Press
295 Kennedy Memorial Drive
Waterville, ME   04901